Translated Language Learning

Alice's Adventures in Wonderland

不思議の国のアリスの冒険

Lewis Carroll

ルイス・キャロル

English / 日本語

Down the Rabbit Hole
ウサギの穴を下って

Alice was beginning to get very tired
アリスはすごく疲れ始めていました
she was sitting by her sister on the grass bank
彼女は芝生の土手に姉のそばに座っていました
but she had nothing to do
しかし、彼女は何もすることがありませんでした
her sister was reading a book
彼女の妹は本を読んでいました
once or twice Alice peeped into the book
一度か二度、アリスは本を覗き込んだ
but the book had no pictures or conversations in it
しかし、その本には写真や会話はありませんでした
"what use is a book without pictures?," thought Alice
「写真のない本に何の役に立つの?」とアリスは思いました
"why would a book have no conversations?"

「なぜ本には会話がないのだろう?」
but she had other things to consider
しかし、彼女には他にも考慮すべきことがありました
"making a chain of daisies would be a pleasure"
「ヒナギクのチェーンを作るのは楽しいでしょう」
"but is it worth the effort of getting up and picking the daisies??"
「でも、起きてヒナギクを摘む努力はあるのだろうか??
」
this was not so easy to think about
これは考えるのはそれほど簡単ではありませんでした
because the day was making her feel sleepy and stupid
なぜなら、その日は彼女を眠くて愚かに感じさせていたからです
but suddenly her thoughts were interrupted
しかし、突然、彼女の思考が中断されました
a White Rabbit with pink eyes ran close by her
ピンクの目をした白ウサギが彼女のそばを走っていました

There was nothing overly remarkable about the rabbit
ウサギについて過度に注目に値するものは何もありませんでした
and Alice did not think the rabbit remarkable either
そしてアリスはウサギも注目に値するとは思いませんでした
nor did it surprise her when the Rabbit spoke
ウサギが話したときも彼女は驚きませんでした
"Oh dear! I shall be too late!" he said to himself
「あらまあ!もう手遅れだ!」と彼は自分に言い聞かせた
but then the Rabbit did something that rabbits didn't do
しかし、その後、ウサギはウサギがしなかったことをしました
the Rabbit took a watch out of its waistcoat-pocket
ウサギはチョッキのポケットから時計を取り出した
he looked at the time and then hurried on
彼は時間を見て、急いで走りました
Alice got to her feet, in amazement
アリスは驚いて立ち上がった
she had never seen a rabbit with a waistcoat before!
彼女はそれまでチョッキを着たウサギを見たことがありませんでした!
nor had she ever seen a rabbit with a watch!
また、時計をつけたウサギも見たことがありませんでした。
Alice was burning with a new curiosity
アリスは新たな好奇心に燃えていました
and she ran across the field after the Rabbit
そして、ウサギの後を追って野原を横切って走りました
she was just in time to see the rabbit disappear
彼女はちょうどウサギが消えるのを見るのにちょうど間に合いました
the rabbit hopped down into a large rabbit-hole
ウサギは大きなウサギの穴に飛び降りました
In another moment, down went Alice after the rabbit!
次の瞬間、アリスがウサギを追いかけました!

The rabbit-hole went straight on like a tunnel
ウサギの穴はトンネルのようにまっすぐに続いていました
and the tunnel kept going for some distance
そして、トンネルはしばらく続きました
and then the path suddenly dipped down
そして、道は突然下り坂になりました
Alice had not a moment to think about stopping herself
アリスは自分を止めようと考える暇さえありませんでした
she found herself falling down and down and down
彼女は自分がどんどん落ちていくことに気づきました
it seemed as if she had fallen down a very deep well
まるで彼女がとても深い井戸に落ちてしまったかのようだった
Either the well was very deep, or she fell very slowly
井戸が非常に深かったか、または彼女は非常にゆっくりと落ちました
because she had plenty of time to fall
彼女が落ちる時間は十分あったからです
as she was falling she could look all around her
彼女が落ちているとき、彼女は周りを見回すことができました
First, she tried to make out where she was going
まず、彼女は自分がどこに向かっているのかを理解しようとしました
but the well was too dark to see anything
しかし、井戸は暗すぎて何も見えませんでした
then she looked at the sides of the well
それから彼女は井戸の側面を見ました
and she noticed that there were cupboards all around her
そして、彼女は周りに食器棚があることに気づきました
and all around the well were book-shelves
そして井戸の周りには本棚がありました
here and there she saw maps and pictures hung upon pegs
彼女はあちこちで、ペグに掛けられた地図や絵を見まし

た
She took down a jar from one of the shelves as she passed
彼女は通り過ぎるときに棚の一つから瓶を降ろした
the jar was labelled for its content
瓶にはその内容物にラベルが付けられていました
"MARMALADE MADE FROM ORANGES"
「みかんから作るマーマレード」
but, to her great disappointment, the marmalade jar was empty
しかし、彼女が非常に失望したことに、マーマレードの瓶は空でした
she did not want to drop the empty marmalade jar
彼女は空のマーマレードの瓶を落としたくなかった
and her fall was very slow
そして彼女の落下は非常に遅かった
so she managed to put the marmalade jar into one of the cupboards
それで彼女はなんとかマーマレードの瓶を食器棚の1つに入れることができました
Down, down, down she fall!
下、彼女は落ちる！
Would the fall ever come to an end?
この堕落はいつか終わるのだろうか？
There was nothing else to do
他にやることがなかった
so Alice soon began talking to herself
だからアリスは、すぐに独り言を言い始めました
"Dinah will miss me very much tonight, I should think!"
「ダイナは今夜、僕をとても恋しく思うだろう、僕は思うべきだ！」
Dinah was Alice's cat
ダイナはアリスの猫だった
"I hope they'll remember her saucer of milk at tea-time"
「ティータイムに彼女のミルクの受け皿を覚えていることを願っています」
"Dinah, my dear, I wish you were down here with me!"

「ダイナ、愛する人、あなたが私と一緒にここにいてくれたらいいのに！」
Alice felt that she was dozing off
アリスは居眠りをしているように感じました
and then suddenly, thump! thump!
そして突然、ドスン！ゴツン！
down she fell upon a heap of sticks
彼女は棒の山の上に落ちました
and she landed on a pile of dry leaves
そして彼女は乾いた葉の山に着地しました
and finally the long fall down the hole was over
そしてついに、穴への長い落下が終わった
Alice was not a bit hurt
アリスは少しも傷ついていませんでした
and she jumped up within a moment
そして彼女はすぐに飛び上がった
She looked up, but it was all dark overhead
彼女は顔を上げたが、頭上は真っ暗だった
in front of her was another long corridor
彼女の前には、また長い廊下がありました
and the White Rabbit was still in sight
そして、白ウサギはまだ見えていました
he was hurrying down the corridor
彼は廊下を急いでいた
There was not a moment to be lost
一瞬たりとも迷うことはありませんでした
off ran Alice like the wind
風のようにアリスを走らせた
around the corner turned the rabbit
角を曲がったところでウサギが回った
she was just in time to hear the rabbit
彼女はちょうどウサギの声を聞くのに間に合いました
""Oh, my ears and whiskers"
「ああ、私の耳とひげ」
"how late it's getting!"
「もう遅くなってきた！」

She was close behind the rabbit
彼女はウサギのすぐ後ろにいました
she turned around another corner
彼女は別の角を曲がった
but the Rabbit was no longer to be seen
しかし、ウサギはもう見えませんでした
She found herself in a long, low hall
彼女は自分が長くて低いホールにいることに気づきました
the hall was lit up by a row of ceiling lamps
ホールは天井のランプの列で照らされていました
There were doors all around the hall
ホールのいたるところにドアがありました
but all the doors were locked
しかし、すべてのドアは施錠されていました
she walked all the way down one side of the hall
彼女は廊下の片側をずっと歩いていった
and she had walked all the way up the other side of the hall
そして彼女はホールの反対側までずっと歩いてきました
she had tried every door
彼女はすべてのドアを試しました
and she walked sadly down the middle of the hall
そして彼女は悲しそうに廊下の真ん中を歩いていきました
"how am I ever going to get out again?"
「どうやってまた出られるのだろう?」

Suddenly she came upon a little table
突然、彼女は小さなテーブルに出くわしました
the table was made entirely of solid glass
テーブルは全体が無垢のガラスでできていました
There was nothing on the table but a tiny golden key
テーブルの上には小さな金の鍵以外は何もありませんでした
the key might belong to one of the doors!
鍵はドアの1つに属している可能性があります！
but, alas! some of the locks were too large for the keys
しかし、悲しいかな！一部のロックはキーに対して大きすぎました
and for the other locks the key was too small
そして他のロックについては、キーが小さすぎました
but, at any rate, the key opened none of the doors
しかし、いずれにせよ、鍵はどのドアも開かなかった
but what was she to do?
しかし、彼女は何をすべきだったのでしょうか？
she went through the hall again

彼女は再びホールを通り抜けた
and this time she noticed a low curtain
そして今度は低いカーテンに気づいた
behind the curtain was a little door
カーテンの向こうには小さなドアがありました
the door was about fifteen inches high
ドアの高さは約15インチでした
She tried the little golden key in the lock
彼女は鍵の中の小さな金色の鍵を試しました
and to her great delight, the key fit in the lock!
そして、彼女が大いに喜んだことに、鍵は錠に収まりました！
Alice opened the door
アリスはドアを開けた
and she found the door led into a small corridor
そして、ドアは小さな廊下に通じているのを見つけました
the corridor was not much larger than a rat-hole
廊下はネズミの穴ほどの大きさではありませんでした
she knelt down and looked along the corridor
彼女はひざまずいて廊下を見つめた
and she saw the loveliest garden you have ever seen
そして、彼女はあなたが今まで見た中で最も美しい庭を見ました
how she longed to get out of that dark hall
彼女はその暗いホールから出ることをどれほど切望していたか
how she wanted to wander among those bright flowers
彼女はその明るい花の間をさまよいたかった
how cool refreshing those fountains looked
その噴水がさわやかに見えたのはなんとクールだったことでしょう
but she could not even get her head through the doorway
しかし、彼女は戸口から頭を出すことさえできませんでした
"Oh," said Alice, mournfully

「あら」とアリスは悲しそうに言いました
"how I wish I could fold up like a telescope!"
「望遠鏡のように折りたたむことができたらどんなにい
いのに！」
"I think I could fold up like a telescope"
「望遠鏡のように折りたたむことができると思う」
"if I only knew how to begin"
「始め方がわかればいいのに」
Alice went back to the table
アリスはテーブルに戻りました
there was the chance of finding another key
別の鍵を見つけるチャンスがありました
or there might be a book of rules
あるいは、ルールの本があるかもしれません
the book could tell her how to fold up like a telescope
その本は、望遠鏡のように折りたたむ方法を彼女に教え
てくれるかもしれません
This time she found a little bottle
今回は小さなボトルを見つけました
"this bottle certainly was not here before," said Alice
「このボトルは確かに前にはなかった」とアリスは言い
ました
and tied around the neck of the bottle was a paper label
そしてボトルの首に巻かれていたのは紙のラベルでした
the label was beautifully printed in large letters
ラベルは大きな文字で美しく印刷されていました
"DRINK ME"
「飲んで」
"No, I'll look first," she said
「いや、まず見るよ」と彼女は言った
"I'll see whether the bottle is marked as poisonous or not,"
「ボトルが毒物と表示されているかどうか確認します」
because she never forgot the lesson about poison
彼女は毒についての教訓を決して忘れなかったからです
"if a bottle is labelled poisonous, it's bound to disagree with
you"

「ボトルに有毒なラベルが付けられている場合、それは
あなたに同意しないに違いありません」
However, this bottle was not marked as poisonous
しかし、このボトルは有毒とマークされていませんでし
た
so Alice ventured to taste the content of the bottle
そうアリスは思い切ってボトルの中身を味わってみまし
た
she found the liquid quite to her liking
彼女はその液体が自分の好みにかなり合っていると感じ
ました
the drink had a sort of mixed flavour
飲み物は一種の混合フレーバーを持っていました
cherry-tart, custard, and pineapple
チェリータルト、カスタード、パイナップル
roast turkey, toffee, and toast with hot butter
ローストターキー、タフィー、トーストとホットバター
and she soon finished off the bottle
そして彼女はすぐにボトルを飲み干しました
"What a curious feeling!" said Alice
「なんて不思議な感じなの!」とアリスは言いました
"I am folding up like a telescope!"
「望遠鏡のように折りたたまれてる!」
And she was folding up like a telescope indeed!
そして、彼女は本当に望遠鏡のように折りたたまれてい
ました!
She was now only ten inches high
彼女の身長は今やわずか10インチでした
and her face brightened up at her thoughts
そして彼女の顔は彼女の考えに明るくなりました
now she was the the right size for the little door
今、彼女は小さなドアにふさわしいサイズになりました
now she could go into that lovely garden
今、彼女はその美しい庭に入ることができました
soon she stopped getting smaller
すぐに彼女は小さくなるのをやめました

she decided on going into the garden at once
彼女はすぐに庭に行くことにしました
but, alas for poor Alice!
しかし、悲しいかな、かわいそうなアリスにとっては！
she got to the door
彼女はドアに着きました
but she had forgotten the little golden key
しかし、彼女は小さな金の鍵を忘れていました
she went back to the table for the key
彼女は鍵を取りにテーブルに戻った
but she found she could not reach high enough
しかし、彼女は十分に高いところに到達できないことに
気づきました
she could see the key quite plainly through the glass
彼女はガラス越しに鍵をはっきりと見ることができまし
た
she tried to climb up the legs of the table
彼女はテーブルの脚を登ろうとした
but the glass was far too slippery
しかし、ガラスはあまりにも滑りやすかったです
eventually she tired herself out with trying
結局、彼女は努力して疲れ果ててしまいました
and the poor little girl sat down and cried
そして、かわいそうな少女は座って泣きました
Alice spoke to herself rather sharply
アリスはやや鋭く独り言を言いました
"Come, there's no use in crying like that!"
「さあ、そんなに泣いても無駄だよ！」
"I advise you to stop right this minute!"
「今すぐやめるように忠告するよ！」
She generally gave herself very good advice
彼女は一般的に自分自身に非常に良いアドバイスをしま
した
though she very seldom followed her own advice
しかし、彼女は自分のアドバイスに従うことはめったに
ありませんでした

and she sometimes was too harsh on herself
そして、彼女は時々自分自身に厳しすぎることがありま
した
and her words brought tears into her eyes
そして彼女の言葉は彼女の目に涙を浮かべました
Soon her eye fell upon a little glass box
すぐに彼女の目は小さなガラスの箱に落ちました
the little glass box was lying under the table
小さなガラスの箱はテーブルの下に横たわっていました
in the glass box was a very small cake
ガラスの箱の中には、とても小さなケーキが入っていま
した
on the cake some words were beautifully written
ケーキの上には、いくつかの言葉が美しく書かれていま
した
the words had been marked in currants
その言葉はスグリでマークされていました
"EAT ME"
「イート・ミー」
"Well, I'll eat the cake," said Alice
「じゃあ、ケーキを食べちゃうよ」とアリスは言いまし
た
"and if the cake makes me grow larger, I can reach the key"
「そして、ケーキが私を大きくするなら、鍵にたどり着
くことができます」
"and if the cake makes me grow smaller, I can creep under
the door"
「そして、ケーキが私を小さくするなら、私はドアの下
に忍び込むことができます」
"so either way I'll get into the garden"
「だから、いずれにせよ、庭に入るよ」
"and I don't care which of the two happens!"
「そして、どちらが起こっても構わない!」
She ate a little bit of the cake
彼女はケーキを少し食べました
and she anxiously spoke to herself:

そして彼女は心配そうに独り言を言いました。
"Which way? Which way?"
「どっち?どっちに?」
and she held her hand on her head
そして彼女は頭に手を当てました
she wanted to feel which way she was growing
彼女は自分がどちらに成長しているのかを感じたかった
のです
she was quite surprised to find what had happened
彼女は何が起こったのかを知って非常に驚いていました
she had remained the same size!
彼女は同じサイズのままだった!
so this time she doubled her efforts
だから今回は、彼女は努力を倍増させた
and soon she finished off the whole cake
そしてすぐに彼女はケーキ全体を食べ終えました

The Pool of Tears
涙のプール

"This is getting more and more interesting!" cried Alice

「だんだん面白くなっちゃったね!」とアリスは叫びました

You can see she was very surprised

彼女がとても驚いていたのがわかります

"I'm opening out like the largest telescope there ever was!"

「今までで最大の望遠鏡のように、私は開いています!」

"Good-bye, feet! Oh, my poor little feet"

「さようなら、足!ああ、私のかわいそうな小さな足」

"I wonder who will put on your shoes for you now, dears?"

「これからは、誰があなたのために靴を履いてくれるのかな?」

"and I wonder who will put on your stockings?"

「それで、誰が君のストッキングを履くのだろう?」

"I shall be a great deal too far away"

「私はかなり遠く離れてしまうでしょう」

"I won't be able trouble myself about you anymore"

「もう君のことで悩むことは許されない」

Just at this moment her head struck against something

ちょうどこの瞬間、彼女の頭が何かにぶつかった

she had reached the roof of the hall

彼女はホールの屋上にたどり着いていた

in fact, she was now more than two meters tall

実際、彼女の身長は2メートル以上になっていました

and she at once took up the little golden key

そしてすぐに小さな金の鍵を取り上げました

and she hurried off to the garden door

そして彼女は庭のドアに急いで行きました

Poor Alice! There was not much she could do

かわいそうなアリス!彼女にできることはあまりありませんでした

she laid down on one side

彼女は片側に横たわった

and she looked through into the garden with one eye
そして彼女は片目で庭を覗き込みました
but to get through was more hopeless than ever
しかし、それを乗り越えることは、かつてないほど絶望的でした
She sat down and began to cry again
彼女は座り、再び泣き始めました
She went on shedding gallons of tears
彼女は何ガロンもの涙を流し続けました
soon there was a large pool all around her
すぐに彼女の周りには大きなプールができました
and the water reached half-way down the hall
そして水は廊下の半分まで達しました
After a time, she heard a little pattering of feet
しばらくすると、彼女は小さな足のパタパタという音を聞いた
she heard the feet coming from the distance
遠くから足音が聞こえた
and she hastily dried her eyes to see what was coming
そして彼女は急いで目を乾かし、これから何が起こるかを見ました
It was the White Rabbit returning
白ウサギが戻ってきた
he was splendidly dressed
彼は立派な服装をしていました
he had a pair of white gloves in one hand
彼は片手に白い手袋を持っていました
and he had a large feather fan in the other hand
そして、もう片方の手には大きな羽根の扇子を持っていました
He came trotting along in a great hurry
彼は大急ぎで小走りでやって来ました
and he muttered to himself, "Oh! the Duchess, the Duchess!"
そして彼は独り言をつぶやいた。公爵夫人、公爵夫人！」
"Oh! won't she be savage if I've kept her waiting!"

「ああ！もし私が彼女を待たせていたら、彼女は野蛮になるんじゃないの！

When the Rabbit came near her, Alice spoke
うさぎが彼女に近づくと、アリスは話しかけました
but she spoke in a low, timid voice
しかし、彼女は低く、臆病な声で話した
"sir, please stop what you're doing for one moment"
「先生、ちょっとおやめください」
The Rabbit startled violently
ウサギは激しく驚いた
he dropped the white gloves and the feather fan
彼は白い手袋と羽根扇子を落としました
and he scurried away into the darkness as fast as he could
そして彼はできるだけ速く暗闇の中へと急いで逃げていった
Alice picked up the feather fan and gloves
アリスは羽根扇子と手袋を拾い上げました
and she kept fanning herself while she kept talking
そして、彼女は話し続けながら自分自身を扇ぎ続けました

"Dear, dear! How strange everything is today!"
「ああ、ああ！今日は何もかもがなんと奇妙なことでしょう！」
"yesterday things went on just as usual"
「昨日はいつも通りのことだった」
"Was I the same when I got up this morning?"
「今朝起きたときも私も同じだったの？」
"But if I'm not the same, there is another question"
「でも、もし私が同じでないなら、また別の疑問がある」
"Who in the world am I?"
「私はいったい何者なの？」
"Ah, that's the great puzzle!"
「ああ、それは素晴らしいパズルだ！」
As she said this, she looked down at her hands
そう言いながら、彼女は自分の手を見下ろしました
she was wearing one of the rabbits little white gloves
彼女はウサギの小さな白い手袋をはめていました
she hadn't noticed she put the glove on while talking
彼女は話しているときに手袋をはめたことに気づいていませんでした
"How can I have done that?" she thought
「どうしてそんなことができるの？」彼女は思った
"I must be growing small again"
「また小さくなってきたんだろうな」
She got up and went to the table to measure her height
彼女は立ち上がり、テーブルに行って身長を測りました
she found that she was now about half a meter tall
彼女は今、自分の身長が約50メートルであることに気づきました
and she was still shrinking rapidly
そして、彼女はまだ急速に縮小していました
She soon found out what the cause of the shrinking was
彼女はすぐに、縮小の原因が何であるかを見つけました
the feather fan was making her smaller again!
羽根の扇子が彼女を再び小さくしていました！

and she dropped the feather fan hastily
そして彼女は急いで羽根扇子を落としました
she dropped the feather fan just in time to save herself
彼女は自分を救うために、ちょうど間に合った羽根扇子
を落としました
had she fanned herself any longer she would have shrunk
away entirely
もし彼女がこれ以上自分を扇いでいたら、彼女は完全に
縮んでいただろう
"That was a narrow escape!" said Alice
「あれは辛うじての逃げ道だったのに!」とアリスは言
った
and she was a good deal frightened at the sudden change
そして、彼女は突然の変化にかなり怯えていました
but she was very glad to find herself still in existence
しかし、彼女は自分がまだ存在していることに気づき、
とても嬉しかったです
"And now, off to the garden!"
「さあ、庭へ行こう!」
And she ran with all speed back to the little door
そして、彼女は全速力で小さなドアに走って戻った
but, alas! the little door was shut again
しかし、悲しいかな!小さなドアは再び閉まりました
and the little golden key was lying on the glass table again
そして、小さな金の鍵は再びガラスのテーブルの上に転
がっていました
"Things are worse than ever," thought the poor child
「事態はかつてないほど悪化している」と可哀想な子供
は思いました
"I never was so small as this before, never!"
「今までこんなに小さくなったのは初めてだよ、絶対に
!」
As she said these words, her foot slipped
そう言いながら、彼女の足が滑った
and in another moment there was a great splash!
そして次の瞬間、大きな水しぶきが上がりました!

she was up to her chin in salt-water
彼女は顎まで塩水に浸かっていた
Her first idea was that she had somehow fallen into the sea
彼女が最初に考えたのは、どういうわけか海に落ちてしまったということでした
However, she soon realized what she was in
しかし、彼女はすぐに自分が何にいるのかに気づきました
she was in a pool of tears
彼女は涙を流していました
the tears she had wept when she was two meters tall
身長2メートルの時に流した涙

Just then she heard something
ちょうどその時、彼女は何かを聞いた
something was splashing about in the pool
プールで何かが飛び散っていました
the splashing came from a little way off
水しぶきは少し離れたところから来ました
and she swam nearer to see what the splashing was
そして、水しぶきが何であるかを見るために近くまで泳

ぎました
she soon saw that it was only a little mouse
彼女はすぐにそれがただの小さなネズミであることに気
づきました
the little mouse had slipped in to the water too
小さなネズミも水に滑り込んでしまった
Alice thought to herself about the situation
アリスは、その状況について自分に言い聞かせました
"Would it be of any use to speak to this mouse?"
「このネズミに話しかけても、何か意味があるのだろう
か?」
"Everything is so up-side-down down here"
「ここは何もかもがひっくり返っている」
"I should think very likely this mouse can talk"
「このネズミは喋れる可能性が非常に高いと思う」
"at any rate, there's no harm in trying"
「いずれにせよ、やってみても害はない」
So she began trying to talk to the mouse
そこで彼女はネズミと話そうと試み始めました
"Oh Mouse, do you know the way out of this pool?"
「ああ、ネズミ、このプールから出る方法を知っている
か?」
"I am very tired of swimming about here, Oh Mouse!"
「ここを泳ぐのはもううんざりだよ、ああ、ネズミ!」
The mouse looked at her rather inquisitively
ネズミはやや興味津々に彼女を見つめた
the mouse seemed to wink with one of its little eyes
ネズミは小さな目でウインクしているように見えました
but the little mouse said nothing
しかし、小さなネズミは何も言いませんでした
"Perhaps the mouse doesn't understand English," thought
Alice
「もしかしたら、ネズミは英語がわからないんじゃない
か」とアリスは思いました
"I dare say it's a French mouse"
「あえて言うならフレンチマウス」

"perhaps this mouse came over with William the Conqueror"
「もしかしたら、このネズミはウィリアム征服王と一緒
に来たのかもしれない」
So she began again, in French
そこで彼女は再びフランス語で始めました
"Where is my cat?" she asked in French
「私の猫はどこ?」彼女はフランス語で尋ねました
it was the first sentence in her French lesson-book
それは彼女のフランス語の教科書の最初の文だった
The Mouse gave a sudden leap out of the water
ネズミは突然水から飛び出しました
and the mouse seemed to quiver all over with fright
そして、ネズミは恐怖で全身が震えているように見えま
した
"Oh, I beg your pardon!" cried Alice hastily
「ああ、ごめんなさい!」とアリスは急いで叫びました
she was afraid that she had hurt the poor animal's feelings
彼女は自分が哀れな動物の気持ちを傷つけてしまったの
ではないかと恐れていました
"I quite forgot you didn't like cats"
「猫が好きじゃなかったのをすっかり忘れてた」
"I don't like cats!" cried the Mouse in a shrill, passionate
voice
「猫は好きじゃない!」ネズミは甲高い情熱的な声で叫
びました
"Would you like cats, if you were me?"
「もし君が僕だったら、猫が好き?」
Alice comforted the mouse in a soothing tone
アリスはなだめるような口調でマウスを慰めました
"Well, perhaps I would not like cats if I were you either"
「まあ、もし僕が君だったら猫は好きじゃないかもしれ
ないけどね」
"please don't be angry about the mention of cats"
「猫の話に怒らないで」
"And yet I wish I could show you our cat Dinah"
「それでも、私たちの猫ダイナを見せられたらいいのに

」

"if you met her I think you'd take a fancy to cats"
「もし彼女に会ったら、猫に夢中になると思うよ」
"if you could only see her"
「彼女が見えさえすれば」
"She is such a dear, quiet thing"
「彼女はとても愛おしくて静かな人です」
The mouse was shaking all over
ネズミは全身を震わせていました
Alice felt certain the mouse must be really offended
アリスは、ネズミが本当に気分を害しているに違いない
と確信しました
"We won't talk about her any more, if you'd rather not"
「彼女のことはもう話さないよ、もし君が話したくなけ
れば」
"We, indeed!" cried the Mouse
「ほんとうに!」とネズミは叫びました
the mouse was trembling down to the end of its tail
ネズミは尻尾の先まで震えていました
"As if I would talk on such a subject!"
「まるでそんな話をするかのように!」
"Our family always hated cats"
「うちの家族はいつも猫が嫌いだった」
"cats; nasty, low, vulgar things!"
「猫；意地悪で、低く、下品なもの!」
"Don't let me hear the name again!"
「二度と名前を聞かせないで!」
"I won't mention cats again indeed!" said Alice
「もう猫の話はしないよ!」とアリスは言いました
she was in a great hurry to change the subject
彼女は話題を変えるのにとても急いでいました
"Are you... are you fond of dogs?"
「お前は......あなたは犬が好きですか?」
"There is such a nice little dog near our house,"
「家の近くにこんなに素敵な小さな犬がいるよ」
"I should like to show you the little dog!"

「小さな犬を見せてあげたいんだけど！」
"this little dog kills all the rats and...
「この小さな犬はすべてのネズミを殺し、そして...
"oh, dear!" cried Alice in a sorrowful tone
「あら、ねえ！」アリスは悲しそうな口調で叫びました
"I'm afraid I've offended you again!"
「また君を怒らせてしまったんじゃないかしら！」
the mouse was swimming away from her as fast as it could go
ネズミは全速力で彼女から離れて泳いでいました
and the mouse made quite a commotion in the pool
そして、ネズミはプールでかなりの騒ぎを起こしました
So she called softly after the mouse
だから彼女はネズミをそっと呼んだ
"my dear mouse, please come back!"
「親愛なるネズミ、戻ってきてください！」
"and we won't talk about cats"
「そして、猫の話はしない」
"and we don't have to talk about dogs either"
「そして、犬の話をする必要もありません」
When the mouse heard this, it turned around
ネズミはこれを聞くと、振り返りました
and the little mouse swam slowly back to her
そして、小さなネズミはゆっくりと彼女のところまで泳いで戻ってきました
the mouse's face was quite pale
ネズミの顔はかなり青白かった
and the mouse spoke, in a low, trembling voice
そしてネズミは低く震える声で話しました
"Let us get to the shore"
「岸に行こう」
"and then I'll tell you my history"
「それから、私の歴史を話します」
"and you'll understand why it is I hate cats and dogs"
「そして、私が猫や犬が嫌いな理由がわかるでしょう」
It had become high time to go

そろそろ行く時が来ました
because the pool was getting quite crowded
プールがかなり混雑していたからです
other birds and animals had fallen into the pool
他の鳥や動物はプールに落ちていました
there were a Duck and a Dodo
アヒルとドードーがいました
and there was a Lory bird and an Eaglet
そして、ロリーバードとイーグレットがいました
and there were several other interesting looking creatures
そして、他にもいくつかの興味深い生き物がいました
Alice led the way out the pool
アリスはプールから出る道を先導しました
and the whole party of animals swam to the shore
そして、動物の一団は皆、岸まで泳ぎました

A caucus race and a long tail
党員集会とロングテール
They were indeed a funny-looking bunch of animals
彼らは確かに面白そうな動物の集まりでした
and they all assembled on the water's bank
そして、彼らは皆、水辺に集まりました
the birds all had bedraggled feathers
鳥たちは皆、羽毛が生えていました
and the furry animals were soaked through
そして、毛むくじゃらの動物たちはびしょ濡れになって
いました
and all were dripping wet, annoyed and uncomfortable
そして、全員が滴り落ち、濡れ、イライラし、不快でし
た

there was one question that had to be answered first
最初に答えなければならない質問が1つありました
what is the best way for everyone to get dry?
誰もが乾くための最良の方法は何ですか?
They had a consultation about this matter

彼らはこの件について相談しました
soon they were all on familiar terms
すぐに彼らは皆、馴染み深い関係になりました
it was as if she had known them all her life
それはまるで彼女が生涯を通じて彼らを知っていたかの
ようでした
the mouse seemed to be a person of some authority
ネズミは何か権威のある人のようでした
"Sit down, all of you, and listen to me!"
「皆さん、座って、私の言うことを聞いてください!」
"I'll soon make you all dry again!"
「すぐにみんなを乾かしてあげるよ!」
They all sat down at once, in a large ring
彼らは皆、大きな輪になって一斉に座りました
and the little mouse sat in the middle
そして、小さなネズミは真ん中に座っていました
"Ahem!" said the mouse with an important air
「えへん!」ネズミは意味深な雰囲気で言いました
"Are you all ready?"
「準備はいいですか?」
"This is the driest thing I know"
「これは私が知っている中で最も乾燥しているものです
」
"Silence all around, if you please!"
「もしよろしければ、周りを静かにしてください!」
"William the Conqueror was favoured by the pope"
「ウィリアム征服王は教皇に好まれた」
"but he was soon submitted to by the English"
「しかし、彼はすぐにイギリス人に服従した」
"they wanted leaders of late"
「彼らは最近、リーダーを求めていた」
"and they had been accustomed to power and conquest"
「そして、彼らは権力と征服に慣れていた」
"Edwin and Morcar, the Earls of Mercia and Northumbria"
「エドウィンとモルカー、マーシア伯爵とノーサンブリ
ア伯爵」

"Ugh!" said the lori bird, with a shiver
「うわっ!」とロリ鳥は震えながら言いました
"and even Stigand, the patriotic archbishop of Canterbury"
「そして、愛国的なカンタベリー大司教のスティガンド
でさえ」
"he also found it advisable"
「彼もそれが賢明だと思った」
"What did he find advisable?" said the duck
「彼は何を賢明だと思ったの?」とアヒルは言いました
"He found it advisable" the mouse replied rather crossly
「彼はそれが賢明だと思った」とネズミはやや横柄に答
えた
but the duck was not satisfied
しかし、アヒルは満足しませんでした
"of course, you know what 'it' means"
「もちろん、あなたは『それ』が何を意味するか知って
います」
"I know what 'it' is when I find a thing," said the duck
「何かを見つけたときの『それ』が何であるかはわかっ
ているよ」とアヒルは言いました
"it's generally a frog or a worm"
「それは一般的にカエルかミミズです」
"The question is, what did the archbishop find?"
「問題は、大司教が何を見つけたのかということです」
The mouse did not notice this question
マウスはこの質問に気づきませんでした
instead, the mouse hurriedly went on with the speech
それどころか、ネズミは急いでスピーチを続けました
"he found it advisable to go with Edgar Atheling"
「彼はエドガー・アセリングを選ぶのが賢明だと思った
」
"to meet William and offer him the crown"
「ウィリアムに会い、彼に王冠を差し出すために」
the mouse continued, turning to Alice as it spoke
ネズミは続け、話しながらアリスに向き直りました
"How are you getting on now, my dear?"

「今はどうですか、お母さん?」
"As wet as ever," said Alice in a melancholy tone
「相変わらず濡れてるわ」とアリスは憂鬱な口調で言いました
"this story doesn't seem to dry me at all"
「この話は私をまったく乾かしていないようです」
"In that case," said the dodo solemnly, rising to its feet
「それなら」ドードーは厳粛に言い、立ち上がりました
"I vote that the meeting be adjourned"
「私は会議を延期することに投票します」
"and I propose an immediate adoption of more energetic remedies"
「そして、私はより精力的な治療法を直ちに採用することを提案します」
"Speak real words!" said the eaglet
「本当の言葉を話せ!」とワシは言いました
"I don't know the meaning of half of those long words"
「あの長い言葉の半分の意味がわからない」
"and, what's more, I don't believe you know either!"
「それに、君も知らないと思うよ!」
"What I was going to say," said the dodo in an offended tone
「何を言おうと思っていたんだ」とドードーは気分を害した口調で言いました
"the best thing to get us dry would be a caucus-race"
「私たちを乾かすのに最適なのは、党員集会です」
"What is a caucus-race?" said Alice
「党員集会って何?」とアリスは言った

"Well," said the dodo, "the best way to explain it is to do it"
「まあ」とドードーは言いました、「それを説明する最良の方法は、それをやることです。」
"First the dodo marked out a race-course"
「まず、ドードーが競馬場をマークした」
"the track was in a sort of circle"
「トラックは一種の円の中にありました」
"and then all the party were placed along the course"
「そして、すべてのパーティーがコースに沿って配置されました」
There was no "One, two, three and away!"
「ワン、ツー、スリー、アウェイ!」などありませんでした。
but they began running when they liked
しかし、彼らは好きなときに走り始めました
and they also finished when they liked
そして、彼らはまた、彼らが好きなときに終了しました
so it was not easy to know when the race was over
そのため、レースがいつ終わったのかを知るのは簡単ではありませんでした
after half an hour or so of running they were all quite dry
30分ほど走った後、彼らはすべてかなり乾いていました
the dodo suddenly called out, "The race is over!"
ドードーは突然「レースは終わった!」と叫びました。

and they all crowded around the dodo
そして、彼らは皆、ドードーの周りに群がりました
all the animals were panting and puffing
すべての動物が息を切らしていました
and they all wanted to know, "But who has won?"
そして、彼らは皆、「しかし、誰が勝ったのか」を知り
たがっていました。
This question the dodo could not immediately answer
この質問にドードーはすぐには答えられなかった
first he had to do a great deal of thinking
まず、彼は多くのことを考えなければなりませんでした
after much thinking, the dodo finally spoke
いろいろ考えた末、ついにドードーが口を開いた
"Everybody has won, and all must have prizes"
「全員が勝った、そして全員が賞品を持っている必要が
あります」
"But who is to give the prizes?" asked a chorus of voices
「でも、誰が賞品をあげるんだ?」と声の合唱が尋ねた
"Well, she, of course," said the dodo
「まあ、もちろん、彼女だよ」とドードーは言った
and the dodo pointed with one finger to Alice
そしてドードーは一本の指でアリスを指しました
and the whole party of animals crowded around her
そして、動物たちの一団全体が彼女の周りに群がってい
ました
they called out, in a confused way, "Prizes! Prizes!"
彼らは混乱した様子で、「賞品だ!賞品!」
Alice had no idea what to do
アリスは何をすべきかわかりませんでした
in despair she put her hand into her pocket
絶望して彼女はポケットに手を入れた
and she pulled out a box of sweets
そして、お菓子の箱を取り出した
luckily the salt-water had not got into the box
幸いなことに、塩水は箱に入っていませんでした
and she handed the sweets around as prizes

そして、お菓子を賞品として渡しました
There was exactly one piece for everyone
みんなにぴったりのピースがありました
The next thing they had to do was to eat the sweets
次にやらなければならなかったのは、お菓子を食べることでした
this caused some noise and confusion
これにより、ノイズと混乱が発生しました
the large birds complained that they could not taste their sweets
大きな鳥たちは、自分たちのお菓子が味わえないと文句を言いました
the small ones choked and had to be patted on the back
小さいものは窒息し、背中を軽くたたいなければなりませんでした
However, it was over at last
しかし、ついに終わってしまいました
and they sat down again in a ring
そして、彼らは再び輪になって座りました
and they begged the mouse to tell them something more
そして、彼らはネズミにもっと何か教えてくれるように頼みました
"You promised to tell me your history, you know," said Alice
「君の歴史を教えると約束したでしょ」とアリスは言った
and she made another little remark about cats in a whisper
そして、彼女はささやき声で猫について別の小さな発言をしました
she didn't want to offend the mouse again
彼女は再びネズミを怒らせたくなかった
the little mouse turned to Alice and sighed
小さなネズミはアリスに向き直り、ため息をついた
"Mine is a long and a sad tale!"
「私の話は長くて悲しい話です!」
"It is a long tail, certainly," said Alice
「確かに、長い尻尾だね」とアリスは言いました

and she looked down with wonder at the mouse's tail
そして、彼女は不思議そうにネズミの尻尾を見下ろしま
した
"but why do you call it a sad tail?"
「でも、なんでそれを悲しい尻尾と呼ぶの?」
And she kept on puzzling about it while the mouse was
speaking
そして、ネズミが話している間、彼女はそれについて困
惑し続けました
so that her idea of the tale was something like this
だから、彼女の物語のアイデアはこんな感じだった

<pre>
        "Fury said to
          a mouse, That
            he met in the
              house, 'Let
                us both go
                  to law: I
                  will prosecute
                  you.——
                    Come, I'll
                  take no denial:
                We must have
              the trial;
            For really
        this morning
      I've
      nothing
      to do.'
        Said the
          mouse to
            the cur,
            'Such a
              trial, dear
                sir, With
                  no jury
                    or judge,
                    would
                    be wasting
                  our
              breath.'
            'I'll be
          judge,
        I'll be
      jury,'
      said
      cunning
        old
        Fury;
          'I'll
            try
              the
                whole
                cause,
                and
                condemn
                you to
      death.'"
</pre>

Fury said to a mouse, That he met in the house"
フューリーはネズミに言った、彼は家で会ったと」
Let us both go to law: I will prosecute you
私たち二人が法律に訴えましょう：私はあなたを起訴し
ます
Come, I'll take no denial: We must have the trial
さあ、私は否定しません：私たちは裁判を受けなければ
なりません
For really this morning I've nothing to do
本当に今朝は何もすることがないんだ
Said the mouse to the cur;
ネズミは呪いに言った。
Such a trial, dear sir, With no jury or judge, would be
wasting our breath
そのような裁判は、親愛なる旦那様、陪審員も裁判官も
いない状態で、私たちの息を無駄にするでしょう
"I'll be judge, I'll be jury," said cunning old Fury
"私は裁判官になる、私は陪審員になるだろう"と狡猾な
古いフューリーは言った
I'll try the whole cause, and condemn you to death
私はすべての原因を試し、あなたを死に追いやる
the mouse spoke severely to Alice
ネズミはアリスに厳しく話しかけました
"You are not paying attention!"
「あなたは注意を払っていません！」
"What are you thinking of?"
「何を考えてるの？」
"I beg your pardon," said Alice very humbly
「ご容赦ください」とアリスはとても謙虚に言いました
"you had got to the fifth bend, I think?"
「5番目の曲がり角にたどり着いたんじゃないかな？」
"You insult me by talking such nonsense!"
「そんな馬鹿げたことを言って、私を侮辱する！」
and the mouse got up and walked away
そして、ネズミは立ち上がって立ち去りました
Alice called after the little mouse

アリスは小さなネズミを呼んだ
"Please come back and finish your story!"
「戻ってきて、あなたの話を終わらせてください!」
And the others all joined in chorus
そして、他のメンバーも全員合唱に参加した
"Yes, please do finish your story!"
「はい、どうかあなたの話を終わらせてください!」
But the mouse only shook its head impatiently
しかし、ネズミは苛立たしげに首を振るだけだった
and the little mouse walked a little quicker
そして、小さなネズミは少し速く歩きました
"I wish I had Dinah, our cat, here!" said Alice
「ここに猫のダイナがいたらいいのに!」とアリスは言いました
This caused a remarkable sensation among the party
これは、党の間で顕著なセンセーションを引き起こしました
Some of the birds hurried off at once
何羽かの鳥が一気に急いで去っていきました
and a Canary called out in a trembling voice, to its children;
そして、カナリアが震える声で子供たちに呼びかけました。
"Come away, my dears!"
「さあ、さあ、私の愛する人たち!」
"It's high time you were all in bed!"
「そろそろみんなベッドに入る時間だよ!」
with various excuses they all went away
さまざまな言い訳をして、彼らは皆去っていきました
and Alice was soon left alone
そしてアリスはすぐに一人残されました
"I wish I hadn't mentioned Dinah!"
「ダイナのことを言わなければよかった!」
"Nobody seems to like her down here"
「ここでは誰も彼女を好きじゃないみたいだ」
"but I'm sure she's the best cat in the world!"
「でも、きっと世界一の猫だよ!」

Poor Alice began to cry again
かわいそうなアリスはまた泣き始めました
because she felt very lonely and low-spirited
彼女はとても孤独で元気がないと感じていたからです
In a little while, however, she again heard something
しかし、しばらくすると、彼女は再び何かを聞いた
a little pattering of footsteps in the distance
遠くで小さな足音がパタパタと音を立てる
and she looked up eagerly
そして彼女は熱心に顔を上げました

It was the white rabbit,trotting slowly back again
それは白ウサギで、再びゆっくりと小走りで戻ってきました
he was looking about anxiously as he went
彼は心配そうに辺りを見回していた
he looked as if he had lost something
彼は何かを失ったかのように見えた
Alice heard him muttering to himself
アリスは彼が独り言をつぶやくのを聞いた
"The Duchess! The Duchess! Oh, my dear paws!"
「公爵夫人！公爵夫人！ああ、私の愛する足！」
"Oh, my fur and whiskers!"
「ああ、私の毛皮とひげ！」
"She'll get me executed, I'm sure of that"
「彼女は私を処刑するだろう、それは確かだ」
"just as sure as ferrets are ferrets!"
「フェレットがフェレットであるのと同じくらい確実です！」

"Where can I have dropped my things, I wonder?"
「どこに物を落としたんだろう?」
Alice guessed in a moment what he was looking for
アリスは彼が探しているものをすぐに推測しました
he was looking for the feather fan
彼は羽根の扇子を探していました
and he was looking for the pair of white gloves
そして、彼は白い手袋を探していました
so she very good-naturedly began looking for the gloves
それで、彼女はとても気さくに手袋を探し始めました
and she looked for the feather fan too
そして、彼女は羽根の扇子も探しました
but the gloves and feather fan were nowhere to be seen
しかし、手袋と羽根扇子はどこにも見当たりませんでした
everything seemed to have changed since her swim in the pool
彼女がプールで泳いで以来、すべてが変わったように見えました
nothing was the same since she had been in the great hall
彼女が大広間にいたときから、何も変わらなかった
and the glass table had vanished
そしてガラスのテーブルは消えていました
and the little door wasn't there either
そして、小さなドアもそこにはありませんでした
Very soon the rabbit noticed Alice
すぐにウサギはアリスに気づきました
he called to her in an angry tone
彼は怒った口調で彼女に呼びかけた
"Mary Ann, what are you doing out here?"
「メアリー・アン、ここで何をしているの?」
"Run home this moment"
「この瞬間に家に帰って」
"and fetch me a pair of gloves and a feather fan!"
「それから、手袋と羽根扇子を持ってきて!」
"and be quick about it!"

「そして、早くやれ！」
Alice spoke to herself as she ran off
アリスは走り去りながら独り言を言いました
"He must have mistaken me for his housemaid!"
「彼は私を彼のメイドと間違えたに違いない！」
"How surprised he'll be when he finds out who I am!"
「彼が私が誰であるかを知ったら、彼はどれほど驚くで
しょう！」
As she said this, she came upon a neat little house
そう言っていると、きれいな小さな家に出くわしました
on the door of the house was a bright brass plate
家のドアには明るい真鍮の皿がありました
"W. RABBIT"
「W. ラビット」
She went in without knocking on the door
彼女はドアをノックせずに中に入った
and she hurried straight upstairs
そして彼女はまっすぐ二階に急いだ
she worried that she might meet the real Mary Ann
彼女は本当のメアリー・アンに会えるかもしれないと心
配していました
because then she would be turned out of the house
なぜなら、そうすれば彼女は家から追い出されるからで
す
and she wouldn't be able to find the feather fan and gloves
そして、彼女は羽根の扇子と手袋を見つけることができ
ません
Alice had found her way into a tidy little room
アリスは整頓された小さな部屋にたどり着きました
in the room was a table by the window
部屋には窓際のテーブルがありました
and on the table was a feather fan
そしてテーブルの上には羽根扇子がありました
and there were two or three pairs of tiny white gloves
そして、小さな白い手袋が二、三組ありました
she picked up the feather fan and a pair of the gloves

彼女は羽根扇子と手袋を拾い上げた
and she was just about to leave the room
そして、彼女はちょうど部屋を出ようとしていました
but then her eyes fell upon a little bottle
しかし、その時、彼女の目は小さな瓶に落ちました
She uncorked the bottle and put it to her lips
彼女はボトルの栓を抜いて唇に当てました
"I do hope it'll make me grow large again"
「それがまた私を大きくしてくれることを願っています
」
"I'm tired of being such a tiny little thing!"
「こんなにちっぽけなものにうんざりだ!」
Alice had hardly drunk half the bottle
アリスはボトルの半分をほとんど飲んでいませんでした
her head was already pressing against the ceiling
彼女の頭はすでに天井に押し付けられていた
and she had to stoop down
そして彼女は身をかがめなければなりませんでした
to save her neck from being broken
彼女の首が折れるのを防ぐために
She hastily put down the bottle
彼女は急いでボトルを置いた
"That's quite enough"
「もう十分だ」
"I hope I don't grow anymore"
「もう成長しないといいなぁ」
Alas! It was too late to wish that!
あああ!それを望むには遅すぎました!
She went on growing and growing
彼女は成長し続けました
and very soon she had to kneel down on the floor
そしてすぐに彼女は床にひざまずかなければなりません
でした
and even then she went on growing
そして、それでも彼女は成長し続けました
as a last resource she put one arm out of the window

最後の手段として、彼女は片腕を窓から出した
and she put one foot up the chimney
そして、片足を煙突に上げました
"Now I can do no more, whatever happens"
「もうこれ以上は何もできない、何が起ころうとも」
"What will become of me?"
「私はどうなるの?」

Alice had a spot of luck
アリスは運が良かった
the little magic bottle had had its full effect
小さな魔法の瓶は、その完全な効果を発揮していた
and Alice grew no larger than she was
そしてアリスは彼女よりも大きくはなりませんでした
After a few minutes she heard a voice outside
数分後、彼女は外で声を聞いた
and she stopped to listen to the voice
そして彼女は立ち止まって声に耳を傾けた
"Mary Ann! Mary Ann!" said the voice
「メアリー・アン!メアリー・アン!」と声が言った
"Fetch me my gloves this moment!"

「今すぐ手袋を持ってきて！」
Then came a little pattering of feet on the stairs
その時、階段で足が少しパタパタと音を立てる音がした
Alice knew it was the rabbit coming to look for her
アリスは、ウサギが自分を探しに来ているのだと知って
いました
and she trembled till she shook the house
そして彼女は家を揺さぶるまで震えました
she quite forgot what her proportions were
彼女は自分のプロポーションが何だったかをすっかり忘
れていました
she was a thousand times as large as the rabbit
彼女はウサギの千倍も大きかった
and she had no reason to be afraid of a rabbit
そして、ウサギを恐れる理由はありませんでした
Presently the rabbit came up to the door
やがてウサギが戸口にやって来ました
and the little rabbit tried to open the door
そして小さなウサギはドアを開けようとしました
the door started to open inwards
ドアが内側に開き始めました
but Alice's elbow was pressed hard against the door
でもアリスの肘はドアに強く押し付けられていました
that attempt proved a failure
その試みは失敗を証明しました
Alice heard the rabbit speak to himself
アリスはウサギが独り言を言うのを聞いた
"Then I'll go around and get in through the window"
「じゃあ、窓から入るよ」
"That you won't!" thought Alice
「そんなことないよ！」とアリスは思いました
and she waited a little again
そして彼女は再び少し待った
soon she heard the rabbit just under the window
すぐに彼女は窓のすぐ下でウサギの声を聞いた
she suddenly spread out her hand

彼女は突然手を広げた
and she made a snatch in the air
そして彼女は空中でひったくりをしました
She did not get hold of anything
彼女は何も持っていませんでした
but she heard a little shriek and a fall
しかし、彼女は小さな悲鳴と転倒を聞いた
and she heard a crash of broken glass
そして、ガラスが割れる音が聞こえた
perhaps the rabbit had fallen
もしかしたらウサギが落ちてしまったのかもしれない
maybe he was in a green-house
もしかしたら、彼は温室にいたのかもしれません
Next came an angry voice; the rabbit's voice
次に怒った声が聞こえました。ウサギの声
"Pat, where are you?"
「パット、どこにいるの?」
And then came a voice she had never heard before
そして、今まで聞いたことのない声が聞こえてきた
"your honour, I'm here!"
「閣下、私はここにいます!」
"I'm digging for apples"
「りんごを掘ってる」
"Here! Come and help me out of this!"
「ここだ!助けに来て!」
"Now tell me, Pat, what's that in the window?"
「さあ、パット、窓に何があるの?」
"Sure, your honour, I will tell you"
「もちろんです、あなたの名誉のために、私はあなたに
言います」
"it's an arm that's in the window!"
「窓にぶつかった腕だよ!」
"Well, an arm has no business there"
「まあ、腕には関係ない」
"go and take the arm away!"
「行って腕を離しろ!」

There was a long silence after this
この後、長い沈黙が流れました
and Alice could only hear whispers now and then
そしてアリスは時々ささやくことしか聞こえませんでした
and at last she spread out her hand again
そしてついに彼女は再び手を広げました
and she made another snatch in the air
そして彼女は空中で別のひったくりをしました
This time there were two little shrieks
今度は小さな叫び声が二つありました
and there was more sounds of broken glass
そして、ガラスが割れる音も増えました
"I wonder what they'll do next!" thought Alice
「次は何をするんだろうね!」とアリスは思いました
"I wish they would pull me out the window"
「窓から引っ張り出してくれたらいいのに」
She waited for some time
彼女はしばらく待った
but for a while she didn't hear anything more
しかし、しばらくの間、彼女はそれ以上何も聞いていなかった
At last came a rumbling of little wheels
とうとう小さな車輪の音が鳴り響きました
and there came the sound of a good many voices
すると、たくさんの声が聞こえてきました
all the voices were talking together
すべての声が一緒に話していた
She could make out some of the words
彼女はいくつかの単語を聞き取ることができた
"Where's the other ladder?"
「もうひとつのはしごはどこだ?」
"Bill's got the other ladder"
「ビルはもうひとつのはしごを持ってる」
"Bill, come here!"
「ビル、こっちに来て!」

"Will the roof bear the load?"
「屋根は荷物に耐えられるの?」
"Who wants to go down the chimney?"
「誰が煙突を降りたいの?」
"Nay, I shall not! You do it!"
「いや、そんなことはしないよ!やるぞ!」
"Here, Bill!"
「ほら、ビル!」
"The master says you've got to go down the chimney!"
「ご主人様が煙突を降りろって言ってるよ!」
Alice drew her foot as far down the chimney as she could
アリスは足をできるだけ煙突の下に引きました
and then she waited to see what was coming
そして、何が来るのかを待っていました
she heard a little animal scratching and scrambling
彼女は小さな動物が引っ掻き、慌てる音を聞いた
the little animal must be in the chimney
小動物は煙突の中にいるに違いない
then she gave one sharp kick
それから彼女は鋭いキックを1回与えました
and she waited to see what would happen next
そして、次に何が起こるのかを待っていました
she heard a general chorus of voices
彼女は声の大合唱を聞いた
"There goes Bill!" they all said
「ビル、行くぞ!」と全員が言った
then she heard the rabbit's voice alone
それから彼女はウサギの声だけを聞いた
"You by the hedge, catch him!"
「生け垣のそばで、彼を捕まえろ!」
there was another moment of silence
また一瞬の沈黙が訪れた
and then there was another confusion of voices
そして、また声が混乱しました
"Hold up his head, Brandy"
「彼の頭を上げて、ブランディ」

"be careful not to choke him"
「首を絞めないように気をつけて」
"What happened to you?"
「君に何があったの?」
Last came a little feeble, squeaking voice
最後に少し弱々しい、きしむ声が聞こえた
"Well, I hardly know no more"
「まあ、もうほとんどわからない」
"thank you all, I'm better now"
「みんなありがとう、今は良くなった」
"there is one thing I can remember"
「覚えていることが1つある」
"something comes at me like a train in a tunnel"
「トンネルの中の列車のように何かが私に襲いかかる」
"and up I fly like a sky-rocket!"
「そして、私はロケットのように飛ぶ!」
there was a minute or two of silence
一分か二分の沈黙が続いた
and then they began moving about again
そして、彼らは再び動き始めました
and Alice heard the Rabbit speak again
そしてアリスはウサギが再び話すのを聞きました
"A barrowful will do, to begin with"
「そもそも、バローフルでいい」
"A barrowful of what?" thought Alice
「手押し車一杯なの?」とアリスは思いました
But she was not kept in suspense for long
しかし、彼女は長くは不安に陥りませんでした
a shower of little pebbles came through the window
小さな小石のシャワーが窓から入ってきました
and some of the little pebbles hit her in the face
そして、小さな小石の一部が彼女の顔に当たった
Alice was surprised about the little pebbles
アリスは小さな小石に驚いた
all the little pebbles were turning into cakes
小さな小石はすべてケーキに変わっていました

and a bright idea came into her head
そして、彼女の頭に良いアイデアが浮かびました
"I should eat one of these cakes"
「このケーキを一つ食べよう」
"cake is sure to make some change in my size"
「ケーキはきっと私のサイズに何か変更を加えます」
So she swallowed one of the cakes
それで彼女はケーキの一つを飲み込みました
and she was delighted to find that she began shrinking
そして、彼女は自分が縮み始めたことを知って喜んでいました
soon she was small enough to get through the door
すぐに彼女はドアを通り抜けられるほど小さくなりました
she ran out of the house
彼女は家を飛び出しました
a crowd of little animals and birds were waiting outside
外では小動物や鳥の群れが待っていました
all the little birds and animals rushed at Alice
すべての小鳥や動物がアリスに殺到しました
but she ran off as fast as she could
しかし、彼女は全速力で走り去った
and soon she found herself safe in a thick wood
そしてすぐに、彼女は深い森の中で安全であることに気づきました
Alice wandered about in the woods
アリスは森の中をさまよった
and she thought to herself:
そして彼女は心の中で考えました。
"I know what I have to do first"
「まず何をすべきかはわかっている」
"first I have to grow to my right size again"
「まず、再び適切なサイズに成長しなければならない」
"and then I have to find my way into that lovely garden"
「そして、あの美しい庭への道を見つけなければならない」

"I suppose I ought to eat or drink something or other"
「何か食べたり飲んだりすべきだと思う」
"but the question is what should I eat or drink?"
「しかし、問題は、何を食べたり飲んだりすべきかということです。」
Alice looked all around her at the flowers
アリスは周りの花を見回しました
and she looked through the blades of grass
そして彼女は草の葉を通して見ました
but she could not see anything to eat or drink
しかし、彼女は食べたり飲んだりするものを見つけることができませんでした
nothing looked like the right thing to eat or drink
食べたり飲んだりするのに適切なもののようには見えませんでした
There was a large mushroom growing near her
彼女の近くには大きなキノコが生えていました
the mushroom was about the same height as Alice
キノコはアリスと同じくらいの高さでした
She stretched herself up on tiptoes
彼女はつま先立ちで体を伸ばした
and she peeped over the edge of the mushroom
そして彼女はキノコの端から覗きました
her eyes immediately met the eyes of a large blue caterpillar
彼女の目はすぐに大きな青い毛虫の目と合った
the caterpillar was sitting on the top of the mushroom
毛虫はキノコの上に座っていました
and the caterpillar had crossed all his arms
そして、毛虫は彼のすべての腕を交差させていました
and he was quietly smoking a long hookah
そして彼は静かに長い水タバコを吸っていました
and he took not the smallest notice of anything
そして、彼は何にも気にも留めませんでした
and he certainly didn't pay attention to Alice
そして彼は確かにアリスに注意を払っていませんでした

Advice from a caterpillar
キャタピラからのアドバイス

At last the caterpillar took the hookah out of its mouth
とうとう毛虫は水タバコを口から取り出しました
and he addressed Alice in a languid, sleepy voice
そして、物憂げで眠そうな声でアリスに話しかけました
"Who are you?" said the caterpillar
「お前は誰だ?」と毛虫は言いました

Alice replied, rather shyly, "I hardly know, sir"
アリスは、やや恥ずかしそうに、「ほとんどわかりません」と答えました。
"just at the moment it's all a bit..."
「今のところ、それはすべて少し...」
"I know who I was when I got up this morning""
「今朝起きたときの自分が誰だったか知っています」
"but I think I must have changed several times since then"
「でも、あれから何回か変わったんじゃないかな」
"What do you mean by that?" said the caterpillar
「それはどういう意味ですか?」と毛虫は言いました
sternly the caterpillar asked her to explain herself

キャタピラは厳しく彼女に説明を求めました
"I can't explain myself, I'm afraid, sir," said Alice
「自分では説明できないの、怖いの」とアリスは言いました
"because I'm not myself"
「だって僕は僕じゃないから」
"you see, being so many different sizes in a day is very confusing"
「ほら、一日にたくさんの異なるサイズがあると、とても混乱します」
She pulled herself up and said very gravely:
彼女は立ち上がり、非常に重々しく言いました。
"I think you ought to tell me who you are, first"
「まず、自分が何者なのか教えるべきだと思う」
"Why?" said the caterpillar
「どうして?」と毛虫は言いました
Alice could not think of any good reason
アリスは正当な理由を思いつくことができませんでした
and the caterpillar seemed to be in a very unpleasant state of mind
そして、毛虫は非常に不快な精神状態にあるように見えました
so she turned away
だから彼女は背を向けた
"Come back!" the caterpillar called after her
「戻ってこい!」毛虫が彼女を呼びました
"I've something important to say!"
「大事なことがあるんだ!」
Alice turned and came back again
アリスは振り返って、また戻ってきた
"Keep your temper," said the caterpillar
「気を抜かないように」と毛虫は言いました
"Is that all?" said Alice
「それだけ?」とアリスは言った
and she swallowed her anger as well as she could
そして彼女はできる限り怒りを飲み込んだ

"No," said the caterpillar
「いや」と毛虫は言いました
the caterpillar unfolded its arms
キャタピラは腕を広げた
and he took the hookah out of his mouth again
そして彼は再び水タバコを口から取り出しました
and he said, "So you think you're changed, do you?"
そして彼は言いました、「それで、君は自分が変わった
と思っているのか?」
"I'm afraid, I am changed, sir," said Alice
「怖いわ、変わってしまったの」とアリスは言いました
"I can't remember things as I used to remember them"
「昔覚えていたことを覚えられなくて」
"and I don't stay the same size for more than ten minutes!"
「それに、同じサイズで10分以上もいられないんだよ!
」
"What size do you want to be?" asked the caterpillar
「どのくらいのサイズになりたいの?」と毛虫は尋ねま
した
"Oh, I don't particularly mind what size I am," Alice hastily replied
「ああ、僕がどんなサイズでもいいんだよ」とアリスは
急いで答えた
"I just don't like changing size so often, you know"
「サイズを頻繁に変えるのは好きじゃないんだよ」
"I would like to be a little larger, sir"
「もう少し大きくなりたいのですが、先生」
"if you wouldn't mind," added Alice
「もしよろしければ」とアリスは付け加えました
"Ten centimetres is such a wretched height to be"
「10センチというのは、とても悲惨な高さです」
"It is a very good height indeed!" said the caterpillar angrily
「なかなかいい高さだね!」と毛虫は怒って言いました
and he reared itself upright as he spoke
そして彼は話しながら直立しました
he was exactly ten centimetres high

彼の身長はちょうど10センチでした
In a minute or two, the caterpillar got down off the mushroom
1分か2分で、毛虫はキノコから降りました
and he crawled away into the grass
そして彼は草むらに這い去った
as he went away, he made some little remarks
彼が去るとき、彼はいくつかの小さな発言をしました
"One side will make you grow taller"
「片面が背を伸ばす」
"and the other side will make you grow shorter"
「そして、その向こう側はあなたを背が低くする」
"One side of what?" thought Alice to herself
「一面はどうなの?」とアリスは心の中で思いました
"The other side of what?"
「その向こう側は?」
"the side of the mushroom," said the caterpillar
「キノコの側面だ」と毛虫は言いました
it was as if she had asked her question aloud
それはまるで彼女が声に出して質問したかのようだった
and in another moment, he was out of sight
そして次の瞬間、彼は見えなくなってしまいました
Alice remained looking thoughtfully at the mushroom
アリスは思慮深くキノコを見つめたままでした
she was trying to make out which were the two sides of the mushroom
彼女はキノコの両面がどちらであるかを確かめようとしていました
At last she stretched her arms around the mushroom
とうとう彼女はキノコに腕を伸ばしました
and she broke off a bit of the edges
そして、彼女は端を少し折った
"And now, which side is which?" she said to herself
「さて、どちらがどちら側なの?」彼女は自分に言い聞かせました
and she nibbled a little of the right-hand bit

そして、彼女は右手のビットを少しかじった
The next moment she felt a violent blow underneath her chin
次の瞬間、彼女は顎の下に激しい打撃を感じた
her chin had struck her foot!
彼女の顎が彼女の足に当たっていた！
She was a good deal frightened by this very sudden change
彼女はこの突然の変化にかなり怯えていました
she was shrinking very rapidly
彼女は非常に急速に縮小していました
so she quickly ate some of the other bit of mushroom
それで彼女はすぐに他のマッシュルームを食べました
Her chin was pressed very closely against her foot
彼女の顎は彼女の足に非常に密着して押し付けられていました
there was hardly room to open her mouth
彼女の口を開く余地はほとんどなかった
but she did at last manage to open her mouth
しかし、彼女はついに口を開くことができました
and she swallowed a morsel of the left-hand bit
そして彼女は左手のビットを一口飲み込んだ
"my head's been freed at last!" said Alice
「やっと頭が解放されたの！」とアリスは言いました
she looked down at herself
彼女は自分自身を見下ろした
but all she could see was an immense length of neck
しかし、彼女が見ることができたのは、巨大な首の長さだけだった
her neck seemed to rise like a stalk
彼女の首は茎のように立ち上がっているように見えました
and she looked down over a sea of green leaves
そして、緑の葉の海を見下ろしました
"Where have my shoulders gotten to?"
「私の肩はどこに行ったの？」
"And oh, my poor hands, how is it I can't see you?"

「そして、ああ、私のかわいそうな手、どうしてあなたに会えないのですか?」
but her neck did have one benefit
しかし、彼女の首には1つの利点がありました
she could move her head in any direction
彼女は頭をどの方向にも動かすことができました
in fact, she was just like a serpent
実際、彼女はまさに蛇のようでした
she gracefully zigzagged her head down
彼女は優雅に頭をジグザグに下げました
and she moved her head through the trees
そして彼女は木々の間を頭を動かしました
but then she heard a sharp hiss
しかし、その時、彼女は鋭いシューという音を聞いた
and she quickly pulled her head back
そして彼女はすぐに頭を後ろに引いた
a large pigeon had flown into her face
大きな鳩が彼女の顔に飛び込んできた
and the pigeon was violently with its wings
そして鳩は激しく翼を振っていました

"Serpent!" cried the pigeon
「蛇だ！」と鳩は叫んだ
"I'm not a serpent!" said Alice indignantly
「私は蛇じゃない！」とアリスは憤慨して言いました
"Leave me alone!"
「ほっとって！」
"I've tried the roots of trees"
「木の根をやってみた」
"and I've tried hedges," the pigeon went on
「そして、生け垣を試したことがある」と鳩は続けました
"but those serpents! There's no pleasing them!"
「でも、あの蛇たち！彼らを喜ばせるものはありません！」
Alice was more and more puzzled
アリスはますます困惑しました
"As if it wasn't trouble enough hatching the eggs," said the pigeon
「まるで卵を孵化させるのに苦労していなかったかのように」と鳩は言いました
"by night and day I must look out for serpents too!"
「夜も昼も、蛇にも気をつけなきゃ！」
"I had just found the highest tree in the forest"
「ちょうど森で一番高い木を見つけたんだ」
"surely I'd be free from serpents here?"
「きっと、ここでは蛇から解放されるのだろうか？」
"and out comes a serpent from the sky!"
「そして、空から蛇が出てくる！」
"But I'm not a serpent, I tell you!" said Alice
「でも、私は蛇じゃないよ、言っちゃうよ！」とアリスは言いました
"I'm a... I'm a... I'm a little girl," she added rather doubtfully
「私は．．．私は．．．私は小さな女の子です」彼女はかなり疑わしそうに付け加えた
she had after all been going through a lot of changes
結局、彼女は多くの変化を経験してきたのです

"You're looking for eggs," said the pigeon
「卵を探しているんだね」と鳩は言いました
"I know that for a fact"
「それは事実として知っています」
"and what does it matter if you're a little girl or a serpent?"
「それで、あなたが小さな女の子であろうと蛇であろうと、何が問題なの?」
"It matters a good deal to me," said Alice hastily
「それは私にとってとても重要なことなの」とアリスは急いで言いました
"but I'm not looking for eggs, as it happens"
「でも、たまたま卵を探しているわけじゃない」
"and I wouldn't want your eggs anyway"
「とにかく君の卵は欲しくない」
"I don't like my eggs raw"
「生の卵が好きじゃない」
"Well, be off then!" said the pigeon in a sulky tone
「じゃあ、行け!」鳩は不機嫌そうな口調で言いました
and the pigeon settled down again into its nest
そして鳩は再び巣に落ち着きました
Alice crouched down among the trees as well as she could
アリスはできるだけ木々の間にしゃがみ込んだ
her neck kept getting entangled among the branches
彼女の首は枝に絡まり続けていた
every now and then she had to stop and untwist her neck
時々、彼女は立ち止まって首のねじれを解かなければなりませんでした
After awhile she remembered the mushroom
しばらくして、彼女はキノコを思い出しました
she still held the pieces of mushroom in her hands
彼女はまだキノコのかけらを手に持っていた
and she set to work very carefully
そして、彼女は非常に慎重に仕事に取り掛かりました
first she nibbled at one piece
まず、彼女は一枚をかじった
and then she nibbled at the other piece

そして、彼女はもう一片をかじった
sometimes she grew taller
時々彼女は背が高くなりました
and sometimes she grew shorter
そして時々彼女は短くなりました
but finally she achieved her usual height
しかし、ついに彼女はいつもの身長に達しました
she hadn't been her own height for some time
彼女はしばらくの間、自分の背丈ではなかった
so everything felt strange for a while
だから、しばらくの間、すべてが奇妙に感じられました
"The next thing to do is to get into that beautiful garden"
「次にやるべきことは、あの美しい庭園に入ることだ」
"how is that to be done, I wonder?"
「それはどういうことだろうと思うけど?」
As she said this, she came upon an open place
そう言っていると、開けた場所に出くわしました
there was a little house, a bit higher than a metre
1メートルより少し高いところに小さな家がありました
"I wonder who lives in this little house"
「この小さな家には誰が住んでいるのだろう」
"I certainly can't go in as big as I am"
「確かに、こんなに大きくは入れない」
"I would frighten them terribly!"
「私は彼らをひどく怖がらせます!」
so she nibbled at the little mushroom again
それで彼女は再び小さなキノコをかじりました
and soon she brought herself down thirty centimetres
そしてすぐに彼女は自分自身を30センチ下に下げました

<h3 align="center">A pig and some pepper
豚とコショウ</h3>

For a minute or two she stood looking at the house
一分か二分、彼女は立って家を見つめていた
suddenly a footman came running out of the woods
突然、一人のフットマンが森から走って出てきた
he was wearing a special livery uniform
彼は特別な制服を着ていました
judging by his face only, she would have called him a fish
彼の顔だけで判断すると、彼女は彼を魚と呼んだでしょう
and he rapped loudly at the door with his knuckles
そして彼は拳でドアを大声で叩いた
the door was opened by another footman
ドアは別のフットマンによって開けられました
this footman too was wearing a special livery
このフットマンも特別な服を着ていました
this footman had a round face and large eyes like a frog
このフットマンは丸い顔とカエルのような大きな目をしていました

The footman that looked like a fish initiated the ceremony
魚のような姿をしたフットマンが儀式を始めました
he pulled out something from under his arm
彼は脇の下から何かを取り出した
and he pulled out from under his arm an envelope
そして彼は腕の下から封筒を取り出した
and this envelope he handed over to the other footman
そして、この封筒をもう一人のフットマンに手渡しました
in a ceremonious tone he told him the orders
彼は儀式的な口調で命令を告げた
"This message is for the Duchess"
「このメッセージは公爵夫人向けです」
"An invitation from the queen to play croquet"
「女王からのクロケット遊びへの招待」
The footman that looked like a frog repeated the order
カエルのような見た目のフットマンが命令を繰り返した
"from the queen"
「女王陛下より」
"an invitation"
「招待状」
"for the Duchess"
「公爵夫人のために」
"playing croquet"
「クロケット遊び」
Then they both bowed low
それから二人は低くお辞儀をした
and the curls in their wigs got entangled together
そして、彼らのかつらのカールが絡まりました
soon the footman that looked like a fish was gone
すぐに魚のように見えたフットマンは消えました
but the footman that looked like a frog was still there
でも、カエルのようなフットマンはまだそこにいました
he was sitting on the ground near the door
彼はドアの近くの地面に座っていました

he was staring stupidly up into the sky
彼は愚かにも空を見上げていた
Alice went timidly up to the door and knocked
アリスはおそるおそるドアのところまで行き、ノックしました
"There's no use in knocking," said the footman
「ノックしても無駄だ」とフットマンは言った
"and that is for two reasons"
「それには2つの理由があります」
"First, because I'm on the same side of the door as you are"
「まず、僕は君と同じドアの側にいるから」
"secondly, because they're making so much noise inside"
「第二に、彼らは中でとても騒いでいるからです」
"no one could possibly hear you"
「君の声が誰にも聞こえない」
And there certainly was a most extraordinary noise going on within
そして、その中では確かに最も異常な騒音が起こっていました
a constant howling and sneezing
絶え間ない遠吠えとくしゃみ
and every now and then a sound of great crashing
そして時折、大きな衝突音がします
as if a dish or kettle had been broken to pieces
まるで皿ややかんが粉々に砕けたかのように
"How am I to get in?" asked Alice
「どうやって入ればいいの?」とアリスは尋ねました
"Should you get in at all?" said the footman
「そもそも乗るべきですか?」とフットマンは言った
"That's the first question, you know"
「それが最初の質問だよ」
Alice opened the door and went in
アリスはドアを開けて中に入った
The door led right into a large kitchen
ドアは大きなキッチンに通じていました
the kitchen was full of smoke from one end to the other

台所は端から端まで煙でいっぱいでした
in the middle of the kitchen was the Duchess
台所の真ん中には公爵夫人がいました
she was sitting on a three-legged stool
彼女は3本足のスツールに座っていました
and she was nursing a baby
そして彼女は赤ん坊を授乳していました
the cook was leaning over the fire
コックは火に身を乗り出していました
he was stirring a large caldron
彼は大きな大釜をかき混ぜていました
and the caldron seemed to be full of soup
そして、大釜はスープでいっぱいになっているようでした
"There's certainly too much pepper in that soup!" Alice said to herself
「あのスープには確かにコショウが多すぎます!」アリスは自分に言い聞かせました
she said it as best she could without sneezing
彼女はくしゃみをせずにできる限りそれを言いました
Even the Duchess sneezed occasionally
公爵夫人でさえ、時折くしゃみをしました
but the baby's actions were the most noteworthy
しかし、赤ちゃんの行動は最も注目に値しました
the baby was sneezing and howling alternately
赤ちゃんはくしゃみと吠えを交互にしていました
there was not a moment's pause between howling and sneezing
吠え声とくしゃみの間に一瞬たりとも休むことはなかった
There were two creatures in the kitchen that did not sneeze
キッチンにはくしゃみをしない生き物が2匹いました
the cook was too busy to sneeze
コックは忙しくてくしゃみをする余裕がなかった
and the large cat did not seem to mind the pepper
そして、大きな猫はコショウを気にしていないようでし

た
instead, the large cat was grinning from ear to ear
それどころか、大きな猫は耳から耳までニヤニヤしてい
ました
"Please would you tell me," said Alice, a little timidly
「教えてもらえませんか」とアリスは少しおそるおそる
言いました
"why is your cat grinning like that?"
「どうして猫はあんなにニヤニヤしているの?」
"It's a Cheshire-Cat," said the Duchess
「チェシャーキャットです」と公爵夫人は言いました
"and that's why he's grinning from ear to ear"
「だから彼は満面の笑みを浮かべているんだ」
"I didn't know that a Cheshire-Cat always grinned"
「チェシャーキャットがいつもニヤリと笑うなんて知ら
なかった」
"in fact, I didn't know that cats could grin," said Alice
「実は、猫がニヤニヤできるなんて知らなかった」とア
リスは言いました
"there is much you don't know," said the Duchess
「あなたが知らないことはたくさんあります」と公爵夫
人は言いました
"there is much you don't know and that's a fact"
「知らないことがたくさんあり、それが事実です」
Just then the cook took the caldron of soup off the fire
ちょうどその時、コックがスープの入った大釜を火から
下ろしました
and at once she started throwing everything within her reach
そしてすぐに彼女は手の届くところにすべてを投げ始め
ました
she threw everything she could at the Duchess and the babe
彼女は公爵夫人と赤ん坊にできる限りのことを投げつけ
ました
first she threw the fire-irons
最初に彼女は火の鉄を投げました
then she threw a handful of saucepans

それから彼女は一握りの鍋を投げました
and finally she threw the plates and dishes
そして最後に、彼女は皿と皿を投げました
The Duchess took no notice of her
公爵夫人は彼女に気づかなかった
even when she was hit by a plate she did not worry
皿に当たっても、彼女は心配しませんでした
the baby was already howling so much
赤ちゃんはもうあんなに吠えていました
so it was impossible to say whether the blows hurt the baby or not
だから、その打撃が赤ちゃんを傷つけたかどうかはわかりませんでした
"Oh, please mind what you're doing!" cried Alice
「ああ、どうか気をつけて!」とアリスは叫びました
and she jumped up and down in an agony of terror
そして彼女は恐怖の苦しみで飛び跳ねました
the Duchess offered Alice the baby
公爵夫人はアリスに赤ん坊を差し出しました
"Here! You may nurse the baby a bit, if you like!"
「ここだ!もしよろしければ、赤ちゃんを少し授乳してもいいよ!」
and she flung the baby at her as she spoke
そして彼女は話しながら赤ん坊を投げつけた
"I must go and get ready to play croquet with the queen"
「女王様と一緒にクロケットをする準備をしに行かなくちゃ」
and she hurried out of the room
そして彼女は急いで部屋を出た
Alice caught the baby with some difficulty
アリスは赤ん坊を難なく捕まえました
because it was a very odd-shaped little creature
それはとても奇妙な形の小さな生き物だったからです
and the baby held out its arms and legs in all directions
そして、赤ん坊は腕と脚を四方八方に差し出しました
"I better take this child away with me," thought Alice

「この子を連れて行った方がいい」とアリスは思った
"they're sure to kill this baby in a day or two"
「彼らはきっとこの赤ん坊を一日か二日で殺すだろう」
"Wouldn't it be murder to leave this baby behind?"
「この赤ん坊を置き去りにするのは殺人じゃないの?」
She said the last words out loud
彼女は最後の言葉を声に出して言った
and the little thing grunted in reply
そして、小さなものは答えてうめき声を上げました
"you best not turn into a pig, my dear," said Alice
「豚に変身しないでね」とアリスは言った
"or else I'll have nothing more to do with you"
「さもなければ、私はあなたとこれ以上何も関係がなく
なるでしょう」
Alice was just beginning to think to herself:
アリスはちょうど考え始めていました。
"Now, what am I to do with this creature, when I get it
home?"
「さあ、この生き物を家に帰ったら、どうしたらいいの
?」
but then the little creature grunted a little violently
しかし、その時、その小さな生き物は少し激しくうめき
ました
and Alice looked down into its face in some alarm
そしてアリスは何か驚いてその顔を見下ろしました
This time there could be no mistake about it
今回は間違いないでしょう
it was neither more nor less than a pig
それは豚以上でも以下でもありませんでした
so she set the little creature down
だから彼女は小さな生き物を下ろしました
and the little creature trot away quietly into the wood
そして、小さな生き物は静かに森の中へ小走りで去って
いきました
Alice felt quite relieved to see the creature go
アリスは、その生き物が去っていくのを見て、とても安

心しました
Alice was a little startled by seeing the Cheshire-Cat
アリスはチェシャーキャットを見て少しびっくりしました
it was sitting on a bough of a tree a few yards off
それは数メートル離れた木の枝に座っていました
The cat only grinned when it saw her
猫は彼女を見てだけニヤリと笑った
"Cheshire-cat," began Alice, rather timidly
「チェシャーキャット」とアリスはやや臆病そうに話し始めた
"would you please tell me which way I ought to go from here?"
「ここからどちらに行けばいいのか教えてもらえますか？」
"In that direction," the cat said
「その方向だ」と猫は言った
and it waved the right paw around
そして、それは右足を振り回しました
"In that direction lives a maker of hats"
「その方向には帽子の職人が生きています」
and then the cat waved its other paw
そして、猫はもう片方の足を振った
"and in that direction lives a march hare"
「そして、その方向には三月うさぎが住んでいます」
"Visit either you like; they're both mad"
「どちらかお好きなところにお越しください。二人とも狂ってる」
"But I don't want to go among mad people," Alice remarked
「でも、おかしい人たちの中には行きたくない」とアリスは言いました
"Oh, you can't help that," said the Cat
「ああ、それは仕方ないよ」と猫は言いました
"we're all mad here"
「私たちは皆、ここで怒っています」
"are you playing croquet with the queen today?"

「今日は女王とクロケットをしますか?」
"I would like to very much," said Alice
「とてもしたいです」とアリスは言いました
"but I haven't been invited yet"
「でも、まだ招待されてないんだ」
"You'll see me there," said the Cat
「そこにいるよ」と猫は言いました
and from one moment to the next the cat vanished
そして、ある瞬間から次の瞬間に猫は消えました
soon Alice got in sight of the house of the march hare
やがてアリスはうさぎの家が見えてきました
this was a very large house
これはとても大きな家でした
so Alice did not want to go near the house
だからアリスは家の近くに行きたくなかった
first she had to nibble some more of the left side bit of
mushroom
まず、彼女は左側のキノコをもう少しかじらなければな
りませんでした

a mad tea-party
狂ったお茶会

In front of the house there was a tree
家の前には木がありました
and under the tree there was a table
そして木の下にはテーブルがありました
and the table was set with all sorts of cutlery
そして、テーブルにはあらゆる種類のカトラリーが置か
れていました
the march hare and the hat maker were at the table
三月うさぎと帽子職人がテーブルにいました
and together they were having tea
そして、彼らは一緒にお茶を飲んでいました
a dormouse was sitting between them
ヤマネが二人の間に座っていました
and the dormouse was fast asleep
そしてヤマネはぐっすり眠っていました
The table was of extraordinary size
テーブルはとてつもなくの大きさでした
but most of the table was unoccupied
しかし、テーブルの大部分は空いていました
they sat crowded together at one corner of the table
彼らはテーブルの片隅にぎっしりと座っていました
and yet they made excuses when they saw Alice
それでも、彼らはアリスを見ると言い訳をしました
"No room! No room!" they cried out
「部屋がない！部屋がない！」と彼らは叫びました
"There's plenty of room!" said Alice indignantly
「部屋はたっぷりあるよ！」とアリスは憤慨して言いま
した
at one end of the table there was a large arm-chair
テーブルの一方の端には大きな肘掛け椅子がありました
and Alice sat herself in the armchair
そしてアリスは肘掛け椅子に座りました
the hat maker opened his eyes very wide
帽子職人は目を大きく見開いた

he couldn't believe what he was seeing
彼は自分が見ているものが信じられませんでした
but his mind was curious about other things
しかし、彼の心は他のことに興味を持っていました
"Why is a raven like a writing-desk?"
「なぜカラスは書き物机のようなものなの?」
Alice was open to the challenge
アリスは挑戦にオープンでした
"I'm glad they've begun asking riddles"
「なぞなぞを解き始めてよかった」
"I believe I can guess that," she added aloud
「そう思うわ」彼女は声に出して付け加えた
The march hare grew curious about Alice
三月うさぎはアリスに興味を持ち始めました
"Do you really think you can find the answer?"
「本当に答えが見つかると思っているの?」
"I think I can find the answer indeed," said Alice
「確かに答えが見つかると思う」とアリスは言った
"Then you should say what you mean," the march hare went on
「じゃあ、言いたいことを言ってみてね」と、行進のウサギは続けました
"I do say what I mean," Alice hastily replied
「言いたいことは言ってるよ」とアリスは急いで答えました
"at the very least I mean what I say"
「少なくとも、私が言っていることは本気です」
"that's the same thing, you know"
「それも同じだよね」
the dormouse also contributed to the conversation
ヤマネも会話に貢献しました
but the dormouse seemed to be talking in its sleep
しかし、ヤマネは眠りの中で話しているように見えました
"I breathe when I sleep"
「寝るときは息をする」

"I sleep when I breathe!"
「息をすると眠る!」
"you might as well say they are the same too"
「あなたも同じだと言った方がいいかもしれません」
"It is the same thing with you," said the hat maker
「あなたも同じです」と帽子職人は言いました
and he poured a little tea on the dormouse's nose
そしてヤマネの鼻に少しお茶を注ぎました
The Dormouse shook its head impatiently
ヤマネは苛立たしげに首を振った
and again the dormouse spoke, without opening its eyes
そして再びヤマネは目を開けずに話しました
"Of course, of course it is the same"
「もちろん、もちろん同じです」
"that's just what I was going to say myself"
「それは私が自分で言おうとしていたことです」

The hat maker turned to Alice and asked another question
帽子職人はアリスに向き直り、別の質問をしました
"Have you guessed the riddle yet?"
「もう謎を解いたの?」
"No, I give up," Alice conceded
「いや、あきらめちゃう」とアリスは認めた
"What's the answer?" she wanted to know
「答えは?」彼女は知りたかった
"I haven't the slightest idea," said the hat maker
「私には少しもわからない」と帽子職人は言った
"Nor do I know," said the march hare
「私も知らない」と行進のうさぎは言いました
Alice gave a weary sigh
アリスは疲れたため息をついた
"there are better uses of time than riddles without answers"
「答えのないなぞなぞよりも、時間の有効活用法がある
」
"have some more tea," the march hare said to Alice, very
earnestly
「もう少しお茶を飲んでね」と、三月うさぎはアリスに
とても真剣に言いました
Alice was quite offended by the offer
アリスはその申し出にかなり気分を害しました
"I've had not had tea yet," Alice replied
「まだお茶を飲んでないの」とアリスは答えました
"therefore I can't have any more tea"
「だからもうお茶は飲めない」
"You mean you can't have less tea," said the hat maker
「お茶を飲む量を減らすことはできないということです
か」と帽子職人は言いました
"it's very easy to take more than nothing"
「何もしないよりは、もっと簡単に取れる」
At this, Alice got up and walked off
すると、アリスは立ち上がって歩き出しました
The dormouse fell asleep instantly
ヤマネはすぐに眠りに落ちました

and neither of the others took the least notice of her going
そして、他の二人も彼女が行くことに少しも気づかなか
った
though she looked back once or twice
彼女は一度や二度振り返ったが
they were trying to put the dormouse into the tea-pot
彼らはヤマネをティーポットに入れようとしていました
"At any rate, I'll never go there again!" said Alice
「とにかく、もう二度とあそこには行かない！」とアリ
スは言いました。
and she walked her way through the woods
そして彼女は森の中を歩いて行きました
"that was the stupidest tea-party I've ever been to"
「今まで行った中で最も愚かなお茶会だった」
Just as she said this, she noticed something
そう言ったとき、彼女は何かに気づきました
one of the trees had a door leading right into it
木の1本には、その中に入るドアがありました
"That's very interesting!" she thought
「それはとても面白い！」と彼女は思いました
"I think I may as well go through the door"
「ドアを通った方がいいと思う」
And through the door she went
そして、彼女はドアを通って行きました
Once more she found herself in the long hall
彼女は再び長い廊下にいることに気づきました
again she was close to the little glass table
再び彼女は小さなガラスのテーブルの近くにいました
she took the little golden key
彼女は小さな金の鍵を取りました
and she unlocked the door that led into the garden
そして、庭に通じるドアの鍵を開けました
Then she set to work nibbling at the mushroom
それから彼女はキノコをかじり始めました
she had kept a piece of the mushroom in her pocket
彼女はそのキノコの一部をポケットに入れていました

and finally she was about a metre tall
そしてついに彼女の身長は約1メートルになりました
then she walked down the little corridor
それから彼女は小さな廊下を歩きました
and then she finally found herself in the beautiful garden
そして、ついに美しい庭に出ました
and she was among the bright flower and the cool fountains
そして彼女は明るい花と涼しい噴水の中にいました

The queen's croquet ground
女王のクロケット場

A large rose-tree stood near the entrance of the garden
庭の入り口近くに大きなバラの木が立っていました
the roses growing on the tree were white
木に生えているバラは白かった
but there were three gardeners painting the rose
しかし、バラを塗る3人の庭師がいました
they were busily painting the roses red
彼らは忙しくバラを赤く塗っていました
and Alice was watching them paint the roses red
そしてアリスは、彼らがバラを赤く塗るのを見ていました
and suddenly their eyes chanced to fall upon Alice
そして突然、彼らの目がたまたまアリスに落ちました
Alice spoke a little timidly
アリスは少しおずおずと話しました
"Would you tell me, please;"
「教えてもらえますか、お願いします」
"why are you all painting those roses?"
「なんでみんなあのバラを描いているの?」
five and seven said nothing, but looked at two
五と七は何も言わず、二を見た
two spoke, in a low voice
二人は低い声で話した
"Why, the fact is, you see, madam"
「なぜ、事実は、ご覧のとおり、マダム」
"this here ought to have been a red rose-tree"
「これは赤いバラの木だったはずだ」
"and we put a white rose-tree in by mistake"
「そして、私たちは誤って白いバラの木を入れました」
"as you would agree, the queen must not find out"
「君も同意するだろうが、女王陛下は見つけてはいけない」
"else we would all have our heads cut off"
「さもなければ、私たちは皆、首を切り落とされてしま

うでしょう」
"So you see, madam, we're doing our best"
「だからね、マダム、私たちは最善を尽くしています」
card five had been anxiously looking across the garden
カード5は心配そうに庭を見渡していました
At this moment card five called out, "The queen! The queen!"
この瞬間、カード5が叫びました。女王様！」
and the three gardeners instantly scurried away
そして、3人の庭師はすぐに急いで逃げました
and they threw themselves flat upon their faces
そして、彼らは顔を伏せた
There was a sound of many footsteps
たくさんの足音がしました
Alice looked around, eager to see the queen
アリスは周りを見回して、女王に会いたくてたまりませんでした
At the start of the procession were ten soldiers
行列の始まりには10人の兵士がいました
their hands and feet were in the corners
彼らの手と足は隅にありました
and in their hands and feet were clubs
そして、彼らの手と足にはこん棒がありました
next came the ten courtiers
次に来たのは10人の廷臣たちです
the courtiers were ornamented all over with diamonds
廷臣たちは全身にダイヤモンドで飾られていました
After the courtiers came the royal children
廷臣たちの後には、王族の子供たちが来ました
there were ten of the royal children
王室の子供たちは10人いました
and all the royal children were ornamented with hearts
そして、すべての王の子供たちはハートで飾られていました
Next came the guests; mostly kings and queens
次に来たのはゲストでした。主に王と女王

and among the kings and queen Alice saw someone
そして、王様と女王様の間でアリスは誰かを見ました
she saw again the white rabbit she had chased
彼女は追いかけた白ウサギを再び見た
The procession was followed the knave of hearts
行列はハートの小片に続いた
he was carrying the king's crown
彼は王冠を背負っていました
and the king's crown was on a crimson velvet cushion
そして、王の王冠は真紅のベルベットのクッションの上
にありました
and then came the end of this grand procession
そして、この大行列の終わりが来ました
and there at the end were the king and queen of hearts
そして最後には、ハートの王様と女王様がいました
the procession came opposite to Alice
行列はアリスとは反対に来ました
and they all stopped and looked at her
そして、彼らは皆立ち止まって彼女を見た
and the queen said severely, "Who is this?"
するとお妃様は厳しく言いました、「これは誰だ?」
She said it to the Knave of Hearts
彼女はそれをハートのナイフに言った
but he just bowed and smiled in reply
しかし、彼はただお辞儀をして微笑んで答えた
Alice spoke very politely
アリスはとても丁寧に話しました
"My name is Alice, so please your majesty"
「私の名前はアリスです。陛下、お願いします」
but she had other thoughts to herself
しかし、彼女は自分自身に別の考えを持っていました
"they're only a pack of cards, after all!"
「結局のところ、彼らはただのカードのパックです!」
"Can you play croquet?" shouted the queen
「クロケットができる?」と女王は叫びました
The question was evidently meant for Alice

その質問は明らかにアリスに向けられたものでした
"Yes!" said Alice loudly
「うん!」アリスは大声で言った
"Come play then!" roared the queen
「じゃあ、遊びに来て!」女王は吠えました
a timid voice spoke to Alice
臆病な声がアリスに話しかけた
"it's a very fine day!"
「とてもいい日ですね!」
She was walking by the white rabbit
彼女は白ウサギのそばを歩いていました
and the White Rabbit was peeping anxiously into her face
そして白ウサギは心配そうに彼女の顔を覗いていました
"a very fine day indeed," confirmed Alice
「本当にいい日ね」とアリスは確認しました
"Where's the duchess?"
「公爵夫人はどこだ?」
"Hush! Hush!" said the Rabbit
「静かに!「静かに!」とウサギは言いました
"She's under sentence of execution"
「彼女は死刑判決を受けている」
"What is she being executed for?" asked Alice
「彼女は何のために処刑されているの?」とアリスは尋
ねた
"She scuffed the queen's ears," the rabbit began
「彼女は女王の耳を擦った」とウサギは話し始めた
the queen shouted in a voice of thunder
女王は雷鳴のような声で叫んだ
"Get to your places!"
「自分の場所に行け!」
and people began running about in all directions
そして、人々は四方八方に走り回り始めました
and they all tumbled up against each other
そして、彼らは皆、互いにぶつかり合いました
However, they got settled down in a minute or two
しかし、彼らは1分か2分で落ち着きました

and then the game began
そして、ゲームが始まりました
Alice had never seen such a curious croquet ground
アリスはこんなに不思議なクロケット場を見たことがな
かった
the grass was all ridges and furrows
草は全部尾根と畝でした
The croquet balls were real hedgehogs
クロケットボールは本物のハリネズミでした
and the mallets were real flamingos
そして、木槌は本物のフラミンゴでした
and the soldiers stood on their hands and feet
兵士たちは手足で立っていました
because the arches was made from their bodies
アーチは彼らの体から作られたからです
The players all played at once
プレイヤー全員が一度にプレイしました
nobody waited for their turns
誰も彼らの順番を待たなかった
and everyone quarrelled with everyone
そして、誰もが誰とでも喧嘩しました
and all were fighting for the hedgehogs
そして、全員がハリネズミのために戦っていました
soon the queen was in a furious passion
すぐに女王は激情しました
and she started stamping about and shouting
そして彼女は足を踏み鳴らし、叫び始めました
"Chop off his head!"
「彼の頭を切り落とす!」
"Chop off her head!"
「彼女の頭を切り落とす!」
"Chop all their heads off!"
「奴らの頭を全部切り落とす!」
Again Alice thought to herself
アリスはまたもや心の中で思いました
"They're dreadfully fond of beheading people here"

「彼らはここで人々を斬首するのが恐ろしいほど好きで
す」
"the great wonder is that there's anyone left alive!"
「素晴らしい驚きは、生き残った人がいるということで
す！」
She was looking about for some way of escape
彼女は何か逃げ道を探していました
she noticed a curious appearance in the air
彼女は空中に奇妙な外観があることに気づきました
"It's the Cheshire-cat," she said to herself
「チェシャーキャットだ」と彼女は独り言を言いました
"now I shall have somebody to talk to"
「さあ、話し相手がいるよ」
"How are you getting on?" said the cat
「調子はどうだい？」と猫は言いました
"I don't think they play at all fairly," Alice said
「彼らが公平にプレーしているとはまったく思わない」
とアリスは言った
and she had a rather complaining tone
そして、彼女はかなり不平を言う口調をしていた
"they all quarrel so dreadfully"
「みんなひどく喧嘩する」
"one can't hear oneself speak"
「自分の声が聞こえない」
"and they don't seem to play by any rules"
「そして、彼らはどんなルールにも従わないように思え
ます」
the cat asked Alice a question in a low voice
猫は低い声でアリスに質問をしました
"How do you like the queen?"
「女王様はどうですか？」
"I don't like her at all," said Alice
「あの子は全然好きじゃない」とアリスは言った

Alice thought she might as well go back
アリスは戻った方がいいと思った
she wanted to see how the game was going
彼女は試合がどうなっているかを見たかったのです
she went off in search of her hedgehog
彼女はハリネズミを探しに出かけました
The hedgehog was busy fighting another hedgehog
ハリネズミは別のハリネズミと戦うのに忙しかった
this was an excellent opportunity
これは素晴らしい機会でした
she could croquet one hedgehog with the other
彼女は1匹のハリネズミをもう1匹でクロケットすること
ができました
but her flamingo was on the other side of the garden
しかし、彼女のフラミンゴは庭の反対側にいました
the flamingo was rather clumsy
フラミンゴはかなり不器用でした
her flamingo was trying to fly up into a tree
彼女のフラミンゴは木に飛んで行こうとしていました
She caught the flamingo by the leg

彼女はフラミンゴの足をつかんだ
and she tucked the flamingo away under her arm
そして彼女はフラミンゴを腕の下にしまい込みました
that way the flamingo couldn't escape again
そうすれば、フラミンゴは二度と逃げられませんでした
Just then Alice happened to meet the duchess
ちょうどその時、アリスはたまたま公爵夫人に会った
The duchess was now out of prison
公爵夫人は今、刑務所から出ていました
She tucked her arm affectionately under Alice's arm
彼女は愛情を込めてアリスの腕の下に腕を押し込んだ
and then they walked off together
そして、彼らは一緒に歩き去りました
Alice was very glad to find her in such a pleasant temper
アリスは、彼女がこんなに気持ちいい感じでいるのを見
つけて、とてもうれしかったです
She was a little startled, however
しかし、彼女は少し驚いていました
she heard the voice of the duchess close to her ear
彼女は耳の近くで公爵夫人の声を聞いた
"You're thinking about something, my dear"
「君は何か考えているんだね」
"and that makes you forget to talk"
「それで話すのを忘れてしまう」
"The game's going on rather better now," Alice said
「今はゲームがかなり良く進んでいる」とアリスは言っ
た
it was one way of keeping the conversation going
それは会話を続けるための1つの方法でした
"it is so indeed," said the duchess
「確かにそうです」と公爵夫人は言いました
"and the moral of that is this:"
「そして、その教訓はこれです。」
"It is love that does it all!"
「すべてを成し遂げるのは愛です!」
"Love is what makes the world go around"

「愛こそが世界を動かしている」
Alice had another explanation
アリスは別の説明をしました
"it's done by everybody minding his own business!"
「それは、誰もが自分のことを気にしているからだ!」
"Ah, well! You could be right"
「ああ、まあ!君の言う通りかもしれない」
"It all means much the same thing," said the Duchess
「それはすべてほとんど同じことを意味します」と公爵
夫人は言いました
and she dug her sharp little chin into Alice's shoulder
そして彼女は鋭い小さな顎をアリスの肩に食い込ませま
した
"and the moral of that is this"
「そして、その教訓はこれです」
"Take care of the sense"
「感覚を大事にする」
"and then the sounds will take care of themselves"
「そうすれば、音は自然に解決する」
but then the duchess's arm began to tremble
しかし、その時、公爵夫人の腕が震え始めました
Alice looked up and there stood the queen
アリスが顔を上げると、そこには女王様が立っていまし
た
the queen had her arms folded
女王は腕を組んでいました
and she was frowning like a thunderstorm!
そして彼女は雷雨のように眉をひそめていました!
"I give you fair warning," shouted the queen
「私はあなたに公正な警告をします」と女王は叫びまし
た
and she stomped on the ground as she spoke
そして彼女は話しながら地面を踏み鳴らしました
"either your head or her head must be off"
「あなたの頭か彼女の頭がずれているに違いない」
"Take your choice!"

「お好きな方を選んでください!」
"and be quick about it"
「そして、それについて迅速に」
The duchess made her choice
公爵夫人は彼女の選択をしました
and within a moment the duchess was gone
そして一瞬のうちに、公爵夫人は去りました
Then the queen spoke to Alice
それからお妃様はアリスに話しかけました
"Let's go on with the game"
「さあ、ゲームを続けよう」
Alice was too frightened to say a word
アリスは怖くて一言も言えませんでした
and she slowly followed her back to the croquet-ground
そして彼女はゆっくりと彼女の後を追ってクロケット場
に戻った
the whole time the queen quarrelled with the other players
その間ずっと、女王は他のプレイヤーと喧嘩していまし
た
"Chop off his head!"
「彼の頭を切り落とす!」
"Chop off her head!"
「彼女の頭を切り落とす!」
"Chop all their heads off!"
「奴らの頭を全部切り落とす!」
soon all the players were in custody
すぐにすべての選手が拘束されました
only the king, the queen, and Alice remained
王様とお妃様とアリスだけが残りました
Then the queen left, quite out of breath
それから女王は息を切らして去っていきました
and she walked away with Alice
そして彼女はアリスと一緒に立ち去りました
Alice heard the king quietly say something
アリスは王様が静かに何かを言うのを聞いた
"You are all pardoned"

「君たちは皆、恩赦された」
but suddenly there was another cry heard
しかし、突然、別の叫び声が聞こえました
"The trial is beginning!"
「裁判が始まります!」
and Alice ran along with the others
そしてアリスは他の人たちと一緒に走りました

who stole the tarts?
タルトを盗んだのは誰ですか?

The king and queen of hearts were seated
ハートの王様と女王様が座っていました
they were on their throne when Alice arrived
アリスが到着したとき、彼らは王位にいました
there was a great crowd assembled around them
彼らの周りには大勢の人が集まっていました
there were all sorts of little birds and beasts
いろんな小鳥や獣がいました
and there was the whole pack of cards
そして、カードのパック全体がありました
the knave was standing in front of them, in chains
その騎士は鎖につながれて彼らの前に立っていた
and there was a soldier on each side to guard him
そして、彼を守るために両側に兵士がいました
near the King was the white rabbit
王様の近くには白ウサギがいました
he had a trumpet in one hand
彼は片手にトランペットを持っていました
and he had a scroll of parchment in the other hand
そして、もう片方の手には羊皮紙の巻物を持っていました
In the very middle of the court was a table
コートの真ん中にはテーブルがありました
on the table was a large dish of tarts
テーブルの上には大きな皿に盛り込まれたタルトが置かれていました
"I wish they'd get the trial done," Alice thought
「裁判が終わったらいいのに」とアリスは思いました
"then we could eat some of those refreshments!"
「じゃあ、その軽食を食べよう!」

The judge, by the way, was the king
ところで、裁判官は王様でした
and he wore his crown over his great wig
そして、彼は大きなかつらの上に王冠をかぶっていました
"That's the jury-box," thought Alice
「あれが陪審員席だよ」とアリスは思いました
"and those twelve creatures, I suppose they are the jurors"
「そして、その12人の生き物は、彼らが陪審員だと思います」
some were animals, and some were birds
動物もいれば、鳥もいました
Just then the white rabbit cried out
ちょうどその時、白ウサギが叫びました
"Silence in the court!"
「法廷に静寂を!」
"Herald, read the accusation!" said the king

「伝令よ、告発を読め!」と王は言った
the white rabbit blew three blasts on the trumpet
白ウサギはトランペットを3回吹き鳴らしました
then he unrolled the parchment-scroll
それから彼は羊皮紙の巻物を広げました
and he read as follows:
そして、彼は次のように読みました。
"The queen of hearts, she made some tarts,"
「ハートの女王、彼女はタルトを作りました」
"All this she did on a summer day"
「彼女が夏の日にやったことすべて」
"The knave of hearts, he stole those tarts"
「ハートのナイフ、彼はそのタルトを盗んだ」
"And he took those tarts far away!"
「そして、彼はそのタルトを遠くに持っていった!」
"Call the first witness," said the king
「最初の証人を呼んでください」と王は言いました
and the white rabbit blew three blasts on the trumpet
そして、白ウサギはトランペットを3回吹き鳴らしました
"bring the first witness!" he called out
「最初の証人を連れてこい!」彼は叫んだ
The first witness was the hat maker
最初の目撃者は帽子職人でした
he came in with a teacup in one hand
彼は片手にティーカップを持って入ってきた
and he had a piece of bread and butter in the other hand
そして、もう片方の手にはパンとバターを持っていました
"You ought to have finished," said the King
「お前は終わらせるべきだった」と王様は言いました
"When did you begin?"
「いつから始めたの?」
The hat maker looked at the march hare
帽子職人はマーチノウサギを見ました
the march hare had followed him into the court

三月うさぎは彼を追って宮廷に入った
he had walked arm in arm with the dormouse
彼はヤマネと腕を組んで歩いていた
"Fourteenth of March, I think it was," he said
「3月14日だったと思う」と彼は言った
"Give your evidence," said the king
「証拠を出せ」と王様は言いました
"and don't be nervous, or I'll have you executed on the spot"
「そして、緊張しないでください。さもないと、その場
で処刑します」
This did not seem to encourage the witness at all
これは、証人を全く励ましそうにではなかった
he kept shifting from one foot to the other
彼は片方の足からもう片方の足へと動き続けた
and he looked uneasily at the queen
そして彼は不安そうに女王を見ました
and, in his confusion, he bit a large piece out of his teacup
そして、混乱の中、彼はティーカップから大きなピース
を噛みちぎりました
really he meant to bite from his bread and butter
本当は彼はパンとバターを噛むつもりだった
Just at this moment Alice felt a very curious sensation
ちょうどその時、アリスはすごく不思議な感覚を感じま
した
she was beginning to grow larger again
彼女は再び大きくなり始めていました
The miserable hat maker dropped his teacup
惨めな帽子職人は彼のティーカップを落としました
and the bread and butter fell to the ground
そして、パンとバターは地面に落ちました
and he went down on one knee
そして彼は片膝をついて倒れた
"I'm a poor man, your majesty," he began
「私は貧しい男です、陛下」彼は話し始めた
"You're a very poor speaker," said the king
「お前は話すのがとても下手だな」と王様は言いました

"You may go," said the king
「行ってもいいよ」と王様は言いました
and the hat maker hurriedly left the court
そして帽子職人は急いでコートを去りました
"Call the next witness!" said the king
「次の証人を呼べ!」と王様は言いました
The next witness was the duchess's cook
次の証人は公爵夫人の料理人でした
She carried the pepper-box in her hand
彼女は手にペッパーボックスを持っていました
and the people near the door began sneezing all at once
そして、ドアの近くにいた人々が一斉にくしゃみを始め
ました
"Give your evidence," said the king
「証拠を出せ」と王様は言いました
"I shall give no evidence," said the cook
「証拠は出さないよ」とコックは言った
The king looked anxiously at the white rabbit
王様は心配そうに白ウサギを見つめました
and the white rabbit spoke in a quiet voice
そして白ウサギは静かな声で話しました
"your majesty must cross-examine this witness"
「陛下はこの証人を尋問しなければなりません」
"Well, if I must, I must," the king said
「まあ、もしそうしなければならないなら、そうしなけ
ればならない」と王様は言いました
"What are tarts made of?"
「タルトは何でできているの?」
"tarts are made of pepper, mostly," said the cook
「タルトは主にコショウでできています」とコックは言
いました
For some minutes the whole court was in confusion
数分間、裁判所全体が混乱していました
eventually they all settled down again
結局、彼らは再び落ち着きました
but by then the cook had disappeared

しかし、その頃にはコックは姿を消していました
"Never mind!" said the king
「気にしないで!」と王様は言いました
"call to the stand the next witness"
「証言台に次の証人を呼べ」
Alice watched the white rabbit as he fumbled over the list
アリスは、白ウサギが手探りでリストをめくるのを見て
いました
you can imagine her surprise at what she heard next
次に聞いた音に驚いた彼女の姿が想像できます
at the top of his shrill little voice, he called the name "Alice!"
彼は甲高い小さな声で「アリス!」という名前を呼びま
した。

Alice's evidence
アリスの証拠

"Here!" cried Alice
「ほら！」とアリスは叫びました
She jumped up in a great hurry
彼女は大急ぎで飛び上がった
and she tipped over the jury-box
そして彼女は陪審員席をひっくり返しました
and she knocked over all the jurymen
そして彼女はすべての陪審員を倒しました
and they fell on to the heads of the crowd below
そして、彼らは下の群衆の頭に落ちました
Alice was in great dismay
アリスはひどく落胆していました
"Oh, I beg your pardon!" she exclaimed
「ああ、ご容赦ください！」彼女は叫んだ
"The trial cannot proceed," said the king
「裁判は進めない」と王は言った
"the jurymen must get back in their proper places"
「陪審員は適切な場所に戻らなければならない」
he repeated the order with great emphasis
彼は非常に強調して順序を繰り返しました
and he looked at Alice sternly
そして彼はアリスを厳しく見つめました
"What do you know about these events?" the king asked Alice
「これらの出来事について、あなたは何を知っているの？」と王様はアリスに尋ねました
"I know nothing on the subject," said Alice
「その件については何も知らない」とアリスは言った
The king then read from his book
その後、王は彼の本を読みました
"Rule forty two"
「ルール42」
"All persons more than a mile high are to leave the court"
「1マイル以上の身長の人は全員、裁判所を出ることに

なっている」
"I'm not a mile high," said Alice
「僕は1マイルも高くないよ」とアリスは言った
"Nearly two miles high," said the Queen
「高さは約2マイルです」と女王は言いました

"Well, I refuse to go," said Alice
「うーん、行くのは断る」とアリスは言った
The king turned pale
王様は青ざめました
and he shut his note-book hastily
そして彼は急いでノートを閉じた
"Consider your verdict," he said to the jury
「あなたの評決を考えてみてください」と彼は陪審員に
言った
he spoke in a low, trembling voice
彼は低く、震える声で話した
then the white rabbit spoke
すると白ウサギが口を開いた
"There's more evidence to come yet"
「まだまだ証拠は出ています」

and he jumped up in a great hurry
そして彼は大急ぎで飛び上がりました
"This paper has just been picked up"
「この論文がちょうど取り上げられました」
"It seems to be a letter written by the prisoner"
「囚人が書いた手紙のようです」
He unfolded the paper as he spoke
彼は話しながら紙を広げた
"It isn't a letter, after all"
「やっぱり手紙じゃないんだよ」
"what it was was a set of verses"
「それが何だったかというと、一組の詩だった」
"Please, your majesty," said the knave
「お願いします、陛下」と騎士は言いました
"I didn't write those verses"
「あの詩は私が書いたのではない」
"and they can't prove that I wrote anything"
「そして、彼らは私が何かを書いたことを証明できない
」
"there's no name signed at the end"
「最後に署名された名前はありません」
the king spoke to the knave
王様は騎士に話しかけました
"You must have meant to cause some mischief"
「何か悪戯をするつもりだったんだろうな」
"else you'd have signed your name like an honest man"
「そうでなければ、正直な男のように自分の名前に署名
していただろう」
There was a general clapping of hands
手を叩く声が一斉に上がった
and the king turned to the white rabbit
そして王様は白ウサギに向き直りました
"Read the verses," he ordered
「詩を読め」と彼は命じた
There was dead silence in the court
法廷には静寂が漂っていた

and the white rabbit read out the verses
そして、白ウサギが詩を読み上げました
They told me you had been to her
彼らはあなたが彼女のところに行ったことがあると私に言いました
And they mentioned me to him
そして、彼らは私を彼に紹介しました
She gave me a good character
彼女は私に良い性格を与えてくれました
But she said I could not swim
でも、彼女は私が泳げないと言いました
He sent them word I had not gone
彼は私が行っていないと彼らに知らせを送りました
We know it to be true
私たちはそれが真実であることを知っています
If she should push the matter on, what would become of you?
もし彼女が問題を押し進めたら、君はどうなるの?
I gave her one, they gave him two
私は彼女に1つ、彼らは彼に2つあげた
You gave us three or more
あなたは私たちに3つ以上を与えました
They all returned from him to you
彼らは皆、彼からあなたのところに戻ってきました
although they were mine before
彼らは以前私のものでしたが
If I or she should chance to be
もし私または彼女が万が一だったら
If I or she were involved in this affair
もし私または彼女がこの事件に巻き込まれていたら
He trusts to you to set them free
彼はあなたが彼らを自由にすることを信頼しています
Exactly as we were
まさに私たちがそうであったように
My notion was that you had been
私の考えでは、あなたはそうだった

Before she had this fit
彼女がこの発作を起こす前
An obstacle that came between
間に立ちはだかる障害
Him, and ourselves, and it
彼と私たち自身、そしてそれ
Don't let him know she liked them best
彼女が一番好きだったことを彼に言わないでください
For this must for ever be a secret, kept from all the rest
なぜなら、これは永遠に秘密であり、他のすべての人々
から守られなければならないからです
This secret must remain a secret between yourself and me
この秘密は、あなたと私の間の秘密のままでなければな
りません
the king was very impressed
王様はとても感動しました
"That's the most important piece of evidence we've heard
yet"
「それは私たちがこれまでに聞いた中で最も重要な証拠
です」
"I don't believe those verses carry an atom of meaning,"
objected Alice
「あの詩には意味のかけらもないと思う」とアリスは反
論した
the King had his own opinion on the matter
国王はこの問題について彼自身の意見を持っていました
"If there's no meaning in those words, that saves a world of
trouble"
「その言葉に意味がなかったら、世界が困る」
"then we needn't try to find the meaning"
「それなら、意味を見つけようとする必要はありません
」
"Let the jury consider their verdict"
「陪審員に彼らの評決を考えさせてください」
"No, no!" said the queen
「いや、いや!」と女王は言いました

"Sentencing first—verdict afterwards"
「量刑が先で、評決は後」
"Stuff and nonsense!" said Alice loudly
「くだらないことばかげている!」とアリスは大声で言いました
"how silly it is to sentence the defendant first!"
「被告に最初に判決を下すなんて、なんてばかげているんだ!」

"Hold your tongue!" said the queen, turning purple
「舌を押さえて!」女王は紫色に変わりながら言いました
"I will not hold my tongue!" said Alice
「舌を噛まない!」とアリスは言った
the queen shouted at the top of her voice
女王は声の限りに叫んだ
"chop off her head!"
「彼女の頭を切り落とす!」
Nobody made a movement
誰も動きをしなかった
"Who cares what you say?" said Alice

「誰があなたの言うことを気にするの?」とアリスは言った
she had grown to her full size by this time
この頃には、彼女はフルサイズに成長していました
"You're nothing but a pack of cards!"
「お前はただのトランプだ!」
At this, all the cards rose up in the air
このとき、すべてのカードが空中に浮かび上がりました
and all the cards came flying down upon her
そして、すべてのカードが彼女に飛んできた
she gave a little scream
彼女は小さな悲鳴を上げた
she was half afraid, but also angry
彼女は半分怖かったが、同時に怒っていた
and she tried to fight the cards off of herself
そして、彼女は自分自身からカードを撃退しようとしました
and then she found herself lying on the grass bank
そして、彼女は自分が草の土手に横たわっていることに気づきました
her head was in the lap of her sister
彼女の頭は妹の膝の上にありました
some dead leaves had landed on her face
彼女の顔には枯れ葉が落ちていました
and her sister was gently brushing the leaves away
そして彼女の妹は優しく葉を払い落としていました
"Wake up, Alice dear!" said her sister
「起きて、アリス!」と姉が言った
"what a long sleep you've had!"
「なんて長い眠りだったんだろう!」
"Oh, I've had such a curious dream!" said Alice
「あら、こんなに不思議な夢を見ちゃったの!」とアリスは言いました
And she told her sister all she could remember
そして、彼女は覚えている限りのことを妹に話しました
all the strange adventures that you have just been reading

about
あなたがちょうど読んでいるすべての奇妙な冒険
Alice got up and ran off
アリスは起きて走り去りました
and she thought, while she ran, about her dream
そして、走りながら、自分の夢について考えました
"what a wonderful dream it had been!"
「なんて素晴らしい夢だったんだろう!」